LORA LEIGH

SUBMISSION SEDUCTION

What the critics are saying...

SUBMISSION

"Lora Leigh once again delivers with this powerful story about learning to love again. Not for the faint hearted, this heated romance pushes the boundaries of what is sexually acceptable. You will be sucked into the story and the tension will keep you reading until you reach the final sentence." ~ *Timeless Tales Reviews.*

SEDUCTION

"I really don't think Ms. Leigh has written a bad book. SEDUCTION is the third installment of the Bound Heart Series. It is so emotional. I was happy to see an Alpha man lose control. The chemistry between Jesse and Terrie is so explosive." ~ *Romance Junkies*

An Ellora's Cave Romantica Publication

www.ellorascave.com

Submission & Seduction

ISBN 1843609452, 9781843609452

Cover art by Scott Carpenter

This book printed in the U.S.A. by Jasmine-Jade Enterprises, LLC.

Trade paperback Publication July 2004

Content Advisory:

S - ENSUOUS
E - ROTIC
X - TREME

Ellora's Cave Publishing offers three levels of Romantica™ reading entertainment: S (S-ensuous), E (E-rotic), and X (X-treme).

The following material contains graphic sexual content meant for mature readers. This story has been rated E–rotic.

S-*ensuous* love scenes are explicit and leave nothing to the imagination.

E-*rotic* love scenes are explicit, leave nothing to the imagination, and are high in volume per the overall word count. E-rated titles might contain material that some readers find objectionable—in other words, almost anything goes, sexually. E-rated titles are the most graphic titles we carry in terms of both sexual language and descriptiveness in these works of literature.

X-*treme* titles differ from E-rated titles only in plot premise and storyline execution. Stories designated with the letter X tend to contain difficult or controversial subject matter not for the faint of heart.

Also by Lora Leigh

A Wish, A Kiss, A Dream *(anthology)*
B.O.B.'s Fall (with Veronica Chadwick)
Bound Hearts 1: Surrender
Bound Hearts 4: Wicked Intent
Bound Hearts 5: Sacrifice
Bound Hearts 6: Embraced
Bound Hearts 7: Shameless
Cowboy & the Captive
Coyote Breeds 1: Soul Deep
Dragon Prime
Elemental Desires *(anthology)*
Elizabeth's Wolf
Ellora's Cavemen: Tales from the Temple I *(anthology)*
Feline Breeds 1: Tempting the Beast
Feline Breeds 2: The Man Within
Feline Breeds 3: Kiss of Heat
Law and Disorder 1: Moving Violations (with Veronica Chadwick)
Legacies 1: Shattered Legacy
Legacies 2: Shadowed Legacy
Los Cavernicolas de Ellora: Cuentos del templo 1 *(anthology)*
Manaconda *(anthology)*
Men of August 1: Marly's Choice
Men of August 2: Sarah's Seduction
Men of August 3: Heather's Gift
Men of August 4: August Heat (12 Quickies of Christmas)
Moving Violations: Law and Disorder
Prime Warriors: Dragon Prime
Sealed With a Wish
Wizard Twins 1: Ménage a Magick
Wizard Twins 2: When Wizards Rule
Wolf Breeds 1: Wolfe's Hope
Wolf Breeds 2: Jacob's Faith
Wolf Breeds 3: Aiden's Charity
Wolf Breeds 4: Elizabeth's Wolf

About the Author

℘

Lora Leigh is a 36-year-old wife and mother living in Kentucky. She dreams in bright, vivid images of the characters intent on taking over her writing life, and fights a constant battle to put them on the hard drive of her computer before they can disappear as fast as they appeared. Lora's family, and her writing life co-exist, if not in harmony, in relative peace with each other. An understanding husband is the key to late nights with difficult scenes, and stubborn characters. His insights into human nature and the workings of the male psyche provide her hours of laughter, and innumerable romantic ideas that she works tirelessly to put into effect.

Lora welcomes comments from readers. You can find her website and email address on her author bio page at www.ellorascave.com.

Tell Us What You Think

We appreciate hearing reader opinions about our books. You can email us at Comments@EllorasCave.com.

BOUND HEARTS:

SUBMISSION
&
SEDUCTION

Lora Leigh

SUBMISSION

Dedication

To RC's Ladies, you know who you are.
For all your encouragement and your support.

Chapter One

&

The house was too quiet. She could hear her own footfalls as she walked through it, her own heartbeat as she stared into her coffee. She could feel her fear, closer, stronger than it had ever been before. The new house was so still, the memories that her New York home had held were absent here.

She had moved to be closer to Tess. To try in some way to make up for the cruel, bitter words she had thrown at her daughter. And she had moved to live again. She had hidden from herself and from the memories of her marriage for so many years that she was feeling the deprivation in ever increasing levels. Her family was here. Her sister, her friends. They were all here. With Tess gone, the New York house was too silent, too lonely. Though this one wasn't much different today.

She still wore the cream lace dress she had chosen for the wedding, though the matching wide-brimmed hat had been thrown carelessly on the embroidered chair that sat inside the front entryway. She felt lost in a way she hadn't felt in years. A loneliness she couldn't explain haunted her; needs she couldn't admit to shadowed her mind and her desires. So she thought of Tess instead.

The wedding had been one of the most beautiful Ella had attended in her life. Her daughter, her baby, had made a gorgeous bride. The pervert she had married had looked handsome and darkly seductive.

She ran her fingers over the careful upsweep of her auburn hair, feeling the pinch of hairpins holding it in place. Her hairdresser had followed her orders to the letter. Not a strand of hair had slipped free of its mooring. Her dress hadn't creased, and her silk stockings hadn't dared slip or snag. She looked as well dressed now, six hours after the wedding, as she had when she left that morning.

Thankfully, with the move to Virginia, the damage she had done to the relationship with her daughter was healing. In her shock, in her rage, she had been hurtful to Tess. But, still, she couldn't believe what she had walked in on.

Her hands trembled as heat flooded her face. It had been Jesse, not James, but the likeness was too great. The twins were identical in nearly every way, even to their sexual preferences. Tall and distinguished, with a lean muscular build and dark-toned skin that looked perpetually tanned. Thick, black hair fell along their napes, straight and glossy, tempting the women around them to touch.

Her legs trembled as she sat down at the small, walnut kitchen table. Her fingers trembled as they covered her lips. Her heart pounded with hard, driving beats within her chest. It had been her worst nightmare come to life, except her daughter played the role Ella had played within those dark visions.

Not with Cole, but with James. And there lay the demon that lurked in her mind. Perverse, depraved. She had walked away from her marriage and the life she had fought to build because of her husband Jase's perverse desires. The light spankings she had managed to tolerate, though they had seared her with shame. Being restrained had been easier, though even then, what pleasure had filtered through the experience had been tainted by the fact that she knew, knew what was coming and she knew she couldn't bear it.

Her lack of submission to Jase's needs had finally broken their relationship. She hadn't been able to give him the trust, the control he needed. She had been terrified, knowing instinctively what would come next, who would come next. And she knew she would never be able to maintain her control, her sanity, if James touched her.

He had been at Tessa's wedding. He had watched her with knowing eyes, so green, so wicked, her body had pulsed with depravity. He had shaken her hand, the heat and pleasure of his touch nearly taking her breath. And all the time he had watched her, knew her, tormented her.

She stalked to the glass door that led to the cool, foliage sheltered area of the garden. The slender heels of her shoes created a hollow, lonely tap against the wood of the porch as she moved to the end of the vine-covered shelter. Her hand gripped the thick post, her nails biting into the wood as she fought her anger, her fears for her daughter.

Tess was too much like Jase. Ella had always been afraid of that, especially after the books she had found years ago, hidden in Tess's bedroom. Her desires were extreme, and evidently she had no fear of them. Unlike her mother, who fought the demons, the knowledge of her own needs.

She couldn't get the image of it out of her mind. She couldn't fight the dark nightmares of James, holding her, taking her as another did. She never knew, never cared who joined them in those nightmare images, all she saw, all she knew, was James.

One day, Ella, you'll have to stop running. When you do, let me know.

"Like hell," she bit out, turning and moving purposely to the house. She wasn't running, and she sure as hell wasn't going to let him know anything.

Jase's sexual tastes had nearly ruined her life, and now they would ruin Tess's. No man could truly love a woman, truly respect her, if he allowed another to touch her, to take her.

She fought the ripple of response between her thighs. The creamy moisture that she fought to ignore, the desires she kept carefully banked, always hidden. Controlled. She couldn't let him break her, couldn't let him see her response to him. If anyone had the power to break her heart, it was James Wyman.

She couldn't ignore him; she couldn't pretend he didn't exist. Due to her own foolishness, he would soon be a daily part of her life. But she could handle it, she assured herself. She had spent her life practicing the careful control that had sustained her over the years. She could handle James Wyman, easily. It was all a matter of control.

Chapter Two

ჽ

It was all a matter of control. James watched as Ella Delacourte led him up the carpet-covered stairs to the bedroom he would be using while he stayed in her home. He was still amazed that she had given into Tess's request that she allow James to stay in the house until the home he was buying was ready to move into.

Her slender waist and gently flared hips drew attention to the delicate, perfect curves of her ass as she moved in front of him. Dressed in gray silk slacks and a pearl gray blouse, she was the epitome of grace and elegance. Calm, controlled…so perfectly controlled it made him itch to hear her scream. To hear that perfectly pitched voice ragged and hot, begging him to fuck her deep and hard, to take her however he wished. He wanted, needed, to break that control.

And Ella knew it. She had been well warned years before, and he wasn't a joking man. But he was a patient man. He had waited five years for the chance at the only woman he knew that could make him think of forever. The only one he knew would challenge his mind, as well as his sexuality. If he could manage to keep from getting kicked out of the house.

He hid his grin. He knew Ella was desperate to make up for the painful words she had thrown at her daughter when she caught her sandwiched between Cole and Jesse. She had been furious, outraged, and if Jesse was right, certain at first that it was James rather than Jesse who had participated in Tess's first ménage.

Tess, too, wanted that relationship repaired, but she also wanted her mother happy. She had been more than happy to participate in James's plot to get closer to her mother.

Especially after he convinced her how long he had been waiting for the opportunity.

"You can use the kitchen and the washroom if you do your own cooking and laundry. The living room is okay for entertaining, but I have to ask that if you need overnight female companionship you rent a motel. I won't have it in my home, James." She pushed open the bedroom door before turning to face him.

She wore only a minimum of makeup today to accentuate her eyes and her graceful cheekbones. Her lips were colored with a soft dawn shade, and at the moment the lower lip appeared slightly swollen, as though she had been biting at it as she walked upstairs.

"I'm not a teenager, Ella." He watched her carefully, aware that her blue eyes were a shade darker than normal, the pupils slightly dilated. He wondered if her pussy was wet, or if she had mastered control over even that part of her body.

"I'm aware of your age," she said coldly. "I'll leave you then to get settled in. If you need anything, the house is laid out fairly simple, and everything is easy to find. I'll talk to you later."

"Ella?" He stopped her as she turned for the door.

He caught the ready, tense set of her body, as though she were preparing herself for a battle. She turned back to him, her expression carefully closed, cool.

"Yes, James?" She kept her voice well modulated, soft yet not simpering.

"Am I allowed to come out of my room if I'm a very good boy?" James kept his voice low, teasing. There was no way in hell he was going to get close to her if she didn't loosen up a little.

She was wary, almost frightened of him, and she almost succeeded in hiding it. Almost. He knew her better than she knew herself in some ways. She stiffened further, her perfectly arched brows snapping into a frown.

"I'm not in the mood for your games." Her voice was non-confrontational, but the flush along her cheekbones warned him of the coming storm. Damn, he loved pissing her off. Watching her eyes glitter in ire, her pale cheeks flushing so prettily. It gave him a glimpse of what she would look like in passion.

He tilted his head curiously. "Shame. Tess assured me you would welcome my company. I'm feeling as though I'm putting you out, Ella. Perhaps I should stay in a hotel until the house is ready."

For a moment—a very brief, infuriating moment—satisfaction glittered in her eyes, until she remembered Tess and her promise to make James comfortable. Her lips thinned as she drew in a deep, careful breath. The smile that she pasted on her face had little to do with warmth; it damned near caused frostbite.

"You're perfectly welcome, James. Tess's little friends are always welcome in my home, you know that."

Ouch. Little friends? He chuckled silently. She was finding every opportunity to remind him that he was several years younger than she was. The six years made little difference to him. As a matter of fact, it seemed perfect. An older man would never keep up with the passions he knew ran beneath that cool exterior.

He allowed a smile to curve his lips as he stared at her intently. "Little friends? I'm hardly that young, Ella."

"Not far from it," she grumbled. "I have work to do, James. Make yourself at home, and perhaps I'll talk to you later."

But not if she could help it.

"What type of work?" He stopped her again. "I was unaware you worked. Jase should have given you a very healthy settlement from the divorce." By God, if he hadn't, James would be talking to him about it.

"That's none of your business." She frowned again. "What I do, James, I do for my own pleasure and how Jase decided to pay me for the divorce is none of your concern."

Pay her for the divorce? James was damned well aware that she was much less than happy in that marriage, yet she sounded bitter, rejected. Had she cared more for Jase than he had once thought? That idea didn't set well in his mind, or in his heart.

"Ella, you weren't happy, and neither was Jase," he said softly.

"I refuse to discuss this with you." She straightened her shoulders majestically, her lips thinning as her anger grew. "I don't mind your presence here, James, but I don't have time to entertain you. You'll have to find your amusements elsewhere."

"But you said no women."

She stopped again as she turned to leave.

"No women." She shook her head tightly, her voice strained. "Not in my home, James. Never again in my home."

Chapter Three

ꟁ

"You know, you need a housekeeper or a cook." James' voice early the next afternoon had her jumping in startled awareness as she finished filling the coffeepot. She turned, facing him, thinking what a shame it was that one man would have such sexual presence.

He stood propped against the doorway, dressed in dark blue silk slacks and a lighter blue silk shirt. His jacket was held at his shoulder by the crook of his finger, and his green eyes regarded her with lustful secrets.

"I'm perfectly capable of cooking my own meals and cleaning my home." She shrugged. She had been raised to do for herself, and cleaning gave her something to do, a way to occupy her hands when her body was filled with restless energy.

He straightened from the doorframe, walking to the table with a casual male grace that threatened to take her breath. She turned quickly from him, moving to the cabinet to retrieve her coffee cup. She fought to still her shaking hands, the nervousness in her stomach that wouldn't seem to go away. She felt immature, like a quaking child before him. It was…unbalancing.

"What if you became busy? Or found a lover?" he asked her then.

Ella fought back her panic. She felt aged, past the time when she could have worried about the future, or a man in her life.

"I'm not looking for a lover, James." She poured her coffee, moving with what she hoped was casual unconcern to the work isle in the center of the room.

She leaned her hip against it, lowering her head as she concentrated on stirring cream and sugar into the dark liquid. She was aware that he was watching her, his eyes dark, intent. She was well aware of his desire for her; a desire she knew wouldn't last beyond the moment. She had no illusions about herself. She was growing older, and her body was slowly showing the signs of it. It wasn't something she worried much about, until she was faced with James. He made her feel young, made her feel desired, and it was dangerous to allow herself to be convinced that it could go further. Too dangerous for her heart.

She watched as he laid the jacket over the back of a chair then moved to the cabinet and snagged a cup for himself. His arm reached up, muscles bunching in his shoulders and back. She shivered, her hands itching to touch him, to feel the strength of motion beneath his flesh.

He turned back to her, leaning against the counter as he regarded her quizzically. "Do you have a lover?"

His voice was whisky rough and dark. It caused arousal to zip along her nerve endings, her skin to become sensitive, needy for his touch. She hated it.

"That's really none of your business." She fought to stay in control. He would leave soon; she knew Jase depended on him at the corporate offices. Not that she understood any of the legal talk she had ever heard in the past, but his job, she knew, was complicated and often required late nights and full days. She was hoping that would keep him out of her hair for the most part.

"Maybe I want to make it my business." His voice hardened imperceptibly as he watched her, his gaze brooding.

Ella couldn't stop the surprise that she knew was reflected on her face. She blinked over at him, her chest tightening in unwanted excitement, her vagina throbbing in unwanted preparation for his touch.

"Why would you want to?" She couldn't understand his desire for her in any way. "I'm not in the market for complications, James. A lover is, by his very nature, a complication."

He tilted his head, his lips quirking in amusement as she raised the coffee cup to her lips.

"Don't you ever get horny, Ella?" She nearly dropped the cup. The coffee she had just taken into her mouth threatened to choke her as it went down the wrong way.

She wheezed, her eyes widening, tearing as she stared at him in shock.

"For God's sake," she bit out when she could breathe again. "Is that any of your business, in any way, James?"

"Actually, it is." He shrugged his shoulders with deceptive laziness. "I want you, Ella. I want to lay you down and touch you in all the ways a man can. I want to fuck you until you're screaming out in agony, because it feels so damned good it hurts. So yeah." He nodded. "It's my business."

The breath lodged in her throat. She felt her cunt cream, her thighs tremble at the thought of him powering into her, fucking her as she screamed. She had never screamed, never wanted anything desperately enough to beg. But she couldn't have James. Anger, directed at herself, at him, poured through her.

She felt her face flush, her body tremble, as she fought for control.

"Sorry, James." She smiled tightly. "I'm really not in the market for a boy toy this year. I guess you just lucked out."

She didn't give him time to reply. Before he could cut her down, before he could tempt her further, she swept from the room, rushing to the safety of her bedroom where her control wasn't as important. Where it wouldn't matter if the tears that filled her eyes escaped. All that mattered was that James didn't know.

Chapter Four

ꟃ

She wouldn't survive this. Ella escaped to her bedroom, locked the door clumsily behind her and stood against it, breathing raggedly. She was flushed, heated, her body tingling. She hated it.

Her fists clenched as she felt her vagina spasm, growing wetter by the second as she remembered the sound of his dark, velvet voice. The deep baritone stroked over her senses then plunged heatedly into her womb. How was she supposed to maintain her control this way? She despised the person she had been while married to Jase. She had acted like a harpy, her fury and fears driving her to rages that had terrified her.

For years. Years she had fought him and what he wanted from her. Because she had known how much he wanted from her. The sexual excesses he enjoyed. She pressed her fists to her stomach, fighting the driving, insidious images that pounded at her brain. She could have tolerated it, she told herself. She could have allowed herself to let go if she hadn't known the man who would eventually arrive.

Jase was nothing if not honest. He had never lied to her when his sexuality had begun emerging. They had been in their early twenties, and his need to dominate, to control her sexual responses had at first seemed merely harmless play. He hated her controlled sexuality. Her fear of letting go, of giving him the responsibility of pleasing her.

Ella had hated his need for it. She had married him because she was pregnant. She had cared for him, had felt a warmth and gentle desire for him, but what he needed she had never wanted. Until she met James. Until she saw in his wicked, knowing eyes, the truth about herself.

God, he had been twenty-six, and she was already in her thirties. She had felt like a cradle robber, looking at him, feeling her pussy gush with moisture, her breasts swelling in desire. And then, she had begun to fantasize. When Jase took her, his cock burrowing into her as he held her to the bed, she imagined it was James.

When he tied her to the bed, her nipples would bead instantly as she thought of James tying her down, thought of James tormenting her body, driving her ragged with need. And when Jase had suggested a ménage, she had thought of James, yet still pretended her husband wasn't truly serious.

Until the day James had walked into the room Jase had set up for his play. Tied to the narrow bed, her legs gaped open, as Jase grew more and more frustrated over her lack of response. James had walked in, his brilliant eyes going to her smooth, bare pussy and she had creamed instantly. She had fought Jase, vowing to never allow him to touch her again. The screaming match that ensued lasted for years. Until the divorce.

She couldn't stand it. For years she had pushed her own needs back, fought to forget James and the terrible desires that raged through her system. Until she walked in and saw Tess with Jesse, James' twin brother. Betrayal had sliced through her soul. And Jesse, damn his black heart, had known. She had seen it in his eyes, in the sardonic lift of his mouth.

Her hand raised to one throbbing breast as the ache in her nipples seemed to only grow. Her fingers glanced over the hard point beneath the silk blouse and sheer bra she wore. Her breath caught on a gasp at the electrified pleasure that washed over her.

She felt her pussy cream furiously, spilling the thick essence along her bare cunt lips. Jase had started her habit of shaving there. It was one of the few things he had taught her that she was thankful for. Until now. Now, the incredible sensitivity of her bare inner lips was a curse. She could feel her juices, hot and slick, coating her flesh as they eased from her vagina, and it only made her ache more.

How was she going to bear having him in her house? Her arms wrapped around her waist as her womb clenched. He hadn't been there an hour yet and already she could think of nothing but his touch moving over her, his hands stroking her, spanking her… She whimpered. She didn't want that, she cried silently, couldn't bear it.

"Ella, you in there? I'm ordering lunch, how do you feel about pizza?" He knocked on her door, startling her into jumping away from it with a tight gasp.

God, wasn't he ever going to leave for work? Surely he wouldn't be here for lunch. She couldn't handle it.

"Fine." She was horrified at the husky, needy quality of her voice. She cleared her throat and swallowed tightly. "I'm tired. You eat. I'm going to lay down."

"Ella, come out and talk to me," he cajoled, his voice soft, filled with such wicked promises she had to bite her lip to keep from calling him to her. "It's just pizza, nothing else." Amusement was like a dark vein of sin in his tone.

She glanced at the clock, then the bedside window. She could find no reasonable excuse to stay hidden in her room, and she knew if she continued to refuse it would only make him suspicious.

"Fine," she bit out, feeling her nails piercing the skin of her palms. "I'll be out in a while. I need to freshen up first."

"I'll be waiting on you. Don't take too long."

As he spoke, Ella tore desperately at her clothes to remove them. She was too hot, too aroused to go to him like this. If she didn't find relief, no matter how minute, she would burn in flames of desire if he so much as brushed against her.

She jerked the drawer of her bedside table open and pulled out the slender, slimline vibrator she had purchased years ago. The soft, supple latex flexed in her palm as she stretched out on her bed. It wasn't thick or long, but buying the damned thing had been one of the hardest things she had ever done in her life.

Her body was already primed, her cunt so wet and sticky that when she ran her fingers through the narrow slit, it clung to her fingers. Her clit was swollen, so large and sensitive she gasped as she circled it with the head of the slender dildo. She eased the control switch on the vibration up, shuddering as the device began to hum.

She couldn't still her gasp of breath as she slid it into the hungry opening of her pussy. Her muscles closed on it, relishing in the hum, but still greedy for more. She pushed it deeper, feeling the sensitive tissue part for the invader.

Ella writhed on the bed, her eyes clenched tightly closed as the fingers of her other hand gripped one of her tight, elongated nipples and pinched lightly.

She couldn't groan, she told herself. She couldn't cry out his name as she had done since seeing him at the wedding and agreeing to let him stay. She couldn't pretend it was James pushing inside her wet pussy, fucking her tight depths. But she couldn't help it either. Her mind formed the image. His body hard and muscular, his cock thick and long as it pushed inside her.

Her control weakened as a small whimper escaped her throat. It wasn't going to be enough. Oh God, she could feel it, the weakness of her body, the incredible arousal searing her nerve endings. She would never achieve a climax hard enough to still the raging pain.

"Let me help you, Ella." The words were like a splash of cold water.

Her eyes flew open to see James, fully dressed, his green eyes glowing with lust as he stared down at her nude, perspiring body. From her breasts to her still slender thighs, spread invitingly as she moved the vibrating dildo inside her pussy.

"Oh God." Embarrassment washed over her as she realized he really was standing there, watching her. He was real this time, not a figment of her imagination.

She would have jumped from the bed if James hadn't moved to stop her, pinning her shoulders to the mattress as he forced her legs closed holding the vibrator inside her pussy as he stared down at her, his powerful legs clamped on the outside of hers as she stared up at him in horror.

His eyes were dark, wicked, his expression filled with sensuality, with lust. Her legs were clamped together as his fingers moved to the control box at her side and he thumbed the power up to its highest level.

Her body jerked in response as the heat flared higher, hotter inside her tormented depths.

"Who do you imagine inside you, Ella?" His voice was deep, rough. "Who's fucking that tight pussy for you, in your mind?"

The deep baritone of his voice stroked over her nerve endings, sending her senses into overdrive. Her hips jerked in reflex, her clit pulsing, throbbing in reaction.

"Don't do this," she cried out, fighting the pleasure as he forced her wrists into one broad hand, holding her securely as he stared into her eyes.

"Is it me, Ella?" he asked her softly. "Do I fuck you in your fantasies? I sure as hell fuck you in mine. Hard and deep, Ella, but my cock is a hell of a lot thicker than that baby pecker you picked. When I push inside you, you're going to be so damned tight you'll come from the pleasure/pain alone. Come for me now, Ella. Come for me baby, so we can discuss this rationally."

Ella couldn't bear it. His voice was enough to make her juices flood her pussy, making the vibration echo along her sensitized flesh.

"I can't." She fought to hold onto her control. She couldn't do this. It was too horrifying, too humiliating. Dear God, how had he opened a locked door?

He leaned closer, his legs loosening from around hers, his hand moving between their bodies as he watched her. She twisted against him as he forced his hand between her slick thighs and gripped the end of the dildo.

"I'm going to fuck you, Ella." He pulled it back as she cried out, staring up at him, seeing his grimace of hot, desperate lust. "Like this." The vibrator was thrust into her pussy, squishing through the thick juices, pounding into her womb as he began to fuck her hard and fast with her own dildo.

Her eyes widened. Her body stiffened as ripples of electricity began to flare through her womb. She could have survived it. She fought for control and it was nearly in her grasp when his head lowered to her nipples.

It had been nearly a decade since a man had touched her. Nearly ten years of fantasizing about this, aching and dreaming of his dominant touch. When his teeth gripped her nipple, his tongue rasping over it as he fucked the vibrator hard and deep inside her pussy, she lost all sense of control.

An orgasm unlike anything she had ever known ripped through her body. She felt the juices spray from her pussy as James groaned, fucking her harder with the latex toy, pushing her thighs apart and heading for her clit. When his lips covered it, his tongue stroked it, she screamed. Her hips arched, her pussy greedily sucking at the vibrator as her clit exploded, and she was flung into a vortex of pleasure that horrified her with its force.

It wouldn't stop. Her upper body jerked from the bed as her muscles contracted, her pussy exploding so hard, so deep, every bone and muscle spasmed in response. She shuddered, feeling the muscles tightening on the vibration inside her as she shook in the grip of her orgasm.

Moments, hours later she collapsed to the bed again, though her womb continued to contract in deep, hard surges as the thick cream flowed from between her thighs.

"There, baby," James soothed her gently and she realized she was crying. His lips feathered over her cheek as he slowly lowered the speed of the vibrator, bringing her back to sanity. She could smell the slight earthy scent of her pussy on his lips, and shuddered at the knowledge of it. "It's okay, baby," he whispered again. "Ease back to me, Ella. It's okay now." He eased back to look at her as the tears welled from her eyes, pouring down her cheeks. "Don't cry, Ella," he whispered gently. "It's okay, baby, it's what we both needed for now."

She shook her head, fighting now to be free of him, to remove the proof of her need, her own perversions from the dripping channel between her thighs. She rolled to her side to escape him, but before she could get away, he pushed her down again, on her stomach, the vibrator once again trapped inside her quaking flesh.

"No, Ella." His voice was hard, tight with lust as his hand smoothed over the quivering cheeks of her rear. "You won't run from it, and by God, I won't let you hide from it any longer." His fingers ran down the cleft of her ass as he hummed in approval.

The juices that flowed from her pussy had slicked the area, giving his fingers greater ease despite the tightening of her muscles.

"James. No," she cried out as he circled the tight opening of her anus. Horror and shame streaked through her system, because despite her embarrassment, she could feel the entrance relaxing, her betraying body sucking at the tip of his finger.

"For now." He was breathing hard at her ear, his chest laboring under his breaths. "For now, Ella. I'll leave you, this time. But you have fifteen minutes to bring that pretty ass out to the living room where we can discuss this with relative sanity. You will not run, Ella. You will not hide. You've come in my mouth now, and I'll be damned, but I won't wait much longer to feel you coming around my cock. Fifteen minutes.

He moved quickly from her, stalking to the door. "And the next fucking time you try to lock a door against me, I'll break the son of a bitch down. Fifteen minutes."

Chapter Five

ꟹ

James was shaking as he stalked to the pristine, perfectly organized living room. His hands, his entire body, were nearly shuddering in reaction, in lust and need, and he feared the loss of his own control. Never. In his entire sexual life his own control had never been so sorely tempted as it had been in Ella's bed, watching her push that pitiful excuse for a dildo inside her tight pussy.

The vibrating toy was slender, soft to the touch, a teaser. A toy to use to drive her to distraction and make her hungry for more, and she didn't even know it. But he intended to do his best to instruct her on the best toys for the job. The job of preparing her, opening her, driving her insane for his final possession.

Jerking the cell phone from his waistband he made a quick call. His eyes watched the door carefully as he put in the order to the online supplier of adult products. A collection of toys, of devices, and he alone would show her the proper use of them.

He wouldn't have long. It would take her five minutes, he guessed, to work herself up. Another five to struggle back into her clothing as she fought the lethargy of her orgasm. Damn. He shook his head as he gave the owner of the adult products store the list. Damn, she had climaxed like nothing he had ever seen. Her pussy had gripped that dildo so tight, so hard, he'd had to struggle to fuck her through the rippling pleasure.

He had watched her abdomen, seeing the convulsive shudders of her womb beneath her flesh as she cried out his name. But she hadn't screamed it, and he swore before the week was over, she was going to scream his name.

He had just flipped the phone close and pushed it back in its slim holder when she stormed into the room.

"You dirty son of a bitch!" she screamed with rage and fear. "You dirty, perverted bastard. This is my home. Mine. And you can fucking leave now."

No control. She flew at him, her face flushed, murder in her eyes, intent on knocking the hell out of him. He didn't think so. He had seen that bruise Jase had sported for a week years before their divorce.

Before she could land the blow he grabbed her wrists, shackling them together in one hand behind her back. His arm went around her waist and he jerked her against him. Before she could curse him again, his lips slanted over hers.

She bit at him, but he nipped at her lip warningly a second before his tongue plunged into her mouth. She was heat and anger, and desperate, hungry lust. She groaned into the kiss, fighting his hold though her lips opened for his tongue, then suckled it tight into her mouth.

James groaned, his cock jerking beneath his zipper at the thought of her mouth enclosing it in such hot pleasure. But for now, his mouth had her, and the taste of her was indescribable. Sweet and warm, filled with the heady, aroused whimpers of a woman overcome with her own desires, pleasured, hungry for more.

He allowed his tongue to stroke the inside of her mouth, to twine with hers as his head slanted, angling closer to allow his lips to stroke hers. She was trembling in his arms, and he knew her pussy would be dripping, wet and aching. And tight. He groaned at the thought of that as he lifted her closer. She had been so tight on that damned slender vibrator that he could barely fuck her with it. She would strangle his cock. His body tensed, his tongue fucking her mouth as she growled in greedy passion beneath his kiss.

He couldn't get enough of her. She arched to him, her breasts unconfined beneath the loose silk shirt she wore, her pants-covered thighs plastered to his as she pressed her mound hard against the thick erection beneath his slacks. The soft cotton pants she wore would do her little good, he promised himself. She would soak them with the juices from her sweet little cunt just as she had the silk slacks.

With a muttered groan he pulled back from the kiss and stared into her face. Her eyes were dazed, her expression slack with sensual need. He could have her now if he was willing to take her. To give her no time for thought, to allow her to believe he had forced the control from her as he had in the bedroom. That would only hurt his intent. It would do nothing to further his own personal goals.

"Enough," he growled, holding onto her as he pushed her into the recliner at his side. "Sit there. And don't get up, Ella, or I promise, you'll regret it," he warned her as she made to do just that.

Evidently she heard the strain of his own fight for control in his voice. She pressed herself tighter against the back of the chair, staring up at him with wide eyes.

James drew in a tight breath. His cock throbbed beneath his pants, pleading for a touch, no matter how timid, no matter how forced. He gritted his teeth and moved back from her.

"Ten years," he bit out, watching her broodingly. "I've wanted you for ten years, Ella, and I'm tired of fighting it."

She shook her head, shock darkening her eyes. "That's not possible." Her voice was thready, desperate.

"Oh, it's more than possible." Disgust welled inside him. "I've wanted you until I could barely breathe, ever since I walked into that damned house of Jase's and saw all that careful control as you fought to give him at least part of what he wanted."

Her face flamed and her eyes looked wild.

"Did you think I couldn't see who you were, Ella? Every time I saw you, you watched me as though you were terrified.

Your nipples would harden, your face would flush, and I knew you wanted me. Me, Ella. And I fought it, fought it just as fucking hard as you did until I walked into that playroom."

He remembered it clearly. Seeing her strapped down on the cot, unaroused, but trying, as Jase fought to pleasure her. He had seen her small cunt; dry yet looking so soft, so tender, as Jase touched it. Then she had seen him. She had fought Jase, screaming at him, crying, but James had watched her cunt. And within seconds it had glistened, her juices spreading over the delicate lips.

He had left. Turned and stalked from the room because he couldn't stand to see her lying there, crying brokenly as she cursed her husband. Jase had given up. He hadn't loved her, and James knew it. What he needed sexually drove him, until he began to bring other women to his bed as his wife moved to the solitary comfort of a downstairs bedroom.

Never in my home. Never again, she had said earlier. He had seen the humiliation flash in her gaze. Jase had brought other women to her home, had taken them to his bed, destroying the pride that was so much a part of her.

"I want you to leave." Her voice quivered as she crossed her arms beneath her breasts, refusing to look at him. "I want you to leave now."

James snorted. "Do you enjoy wasting your breath, Ella? You don't want me to leave. You're just too fucking scared for me to stay."

"No." She shook her head desperately.

"Yes," he all but snarled. "Prove it then. Stand up, Ella, and drop those pants. Let me sink my fingers into that tight cunt and see if you're still wet and ready for me, because I bet you are. I bet you would come again, Ella..."

"Stop it." She jerked to her feet, her voice raspy, hoarse. "You're younger..."

"I'll fuck you harder than any man your own age could ever hope to." He stood in front of her, staring down at her furiously. "Better yet, Ella, I'll fuck you like you need it. I'll make all those nasty little fantasies of yours reality, and then I'll teach you some you could have never imagined."

"I won't listen to this," she raged heatedly. "I let you come into my house as a guest..."

"And I'll come in your pussy as your lover," he bit out, breaking over her outraged declaration. "Your pussy, your mouth, your ass. Wherever I can get my cock in, Ella, I'll fuck you until I can fill every inch of your body with my cum."

She collapsed back in the chair. He could see her trembling, fighting herself as well as him.

"But we both know it's not that easy, don't we, baby?" He stooped in front of her, his hands going to the button of her pants. "We both know that what I want will be more intense, and a hell of a lot more serious than anything Jase ever asked of you, and that's what's scaring the hell out of you."

"James." Her hand covered his as her voice broke. "Don't do this to me, please."

"Don't do what, Ella?" he asked her, tenderness—fuck, *love*—welling inside him so deep, so strong it nearly strangled him. "Don't give you what you need? Don't satisfy your fantasies, your desires? Don't show you how damned good it's going to hurt when my cock pushes inside your tight pussy? Sorry, baby, but I think I just reached the end of my control. I won't let you run anymore."

* * * * *

Ella watched James, seeing the determination in his eyes, the lust that flushed his face, tightened his features, and she couldn't find the words to fight him. She trembled before him instead, her body still weak, still vibrating in longing after the climax he had given her earlier. She needed more. Her thighs trembled, her cunt gushing her juices as she tried to find a way to make him leave.

She could make him. She could call the police and he wouldn't stop her. She could have him thrown out. She could scream if she could find the breath after that kiss. But she knew she couldn't bear to see him dragged away. Couldn't bear the humiliation she knew he would face. But she couldn't give in to him either. She wouldn't give in to him. At least, not entirely.

"Just us," she finally whispered, trembling. "Just sex."

His whole body tightened. She had expected him to finish removing her pants, to give her what she needed. She didn't expect him to draw away from her.

"I take control," he said broodingly. "Whatever I want to give you, Ella, however I want to give it."

"My terms," she bit out desperately, then watched in horror as he shook his head slowly.

"No, Ella. My terms as my woman. Your choice."

Chapter Six

ꝏ

My terms as my woman. Your choice. The words resounded in her head that night and all the next day. James was the head corporate lawyer for Delacourte Electronics, and with the growth of Jase's business, she knew he often put in long hours working, both in the office and at home, she guessed. That left the house silent and lonely that next day.

She wandered through the rooms, tired from the restlessness of her sleep the night before, and torn between her desires and his. She remembered clearly Jase's demented sexual games. Not that any of them made sense to her at the time. What was the purpose in tying a woman down? Unless your fantasy was rape, which he always swore wasn't true. She hadn't had a clue until James walked into that damned room and stared with flaring lust at her naked, bound body.

Ella remembered, clearly, her own agonizing humiliation. Spread open while her husband touched her, as she fought to find arousal in the game he wanted to play. But there had been none. Nothing until James' eyes had centered on her thighs, spearing past her boredom with an instant, flaring heat. She had creamed herself in seconds, and the terror that Jase, or even James would realize it, had nearly destroyed her.

She sighed morosely as she walked out to the back porch and threw herself into one of the padded loungers there. The late afternoon sun was passing over, but beneath the cool shelter of the low trees and thick vines that wrapped around the porch, Ella was spared the blinding heat. The outer heat. Her inner heat was killing her.

She had finally given up on changing panties. After the second pair, she had thrown her hands up in disgust and stopped. After ten years of no sexual activity, of fighting her desires and her needs, her body was evidently taking over. It wouldn't stop producing the hot, slick fluid that would ease James' entrance into her tight pussy. And it was tight. She shuddered in longing. Tight and greedy, anxious to feel James' thick, hard cock sliding into it.

She was losing her mind. She closed her eyes as she tightened her thighs against the empty ache in the center of her body. Her vibrator had disappeared. She didn't know how, or why, but somehow James had managed to steal it, or hide it, because it was no place to be found. And she needed it.

"You look pretty there, Ella." She jumped as James stepped to the doorway, staring at her with those hot, sin-filled eyes.

"What are you doing here? You're supposed to be working." She would have jumped from the lounge chair if he hadn't moved to stand in front of it.

She stared up at him, fighting to control her breathing as well as the desire that shook her to her soul.

"I took the rest of the day off." He shrugged his broad shoulders as he pushed his hands into the pockets of his pants. The action only drew attention to the thick ridge beneath the material. "Is your pussy wet?"

Ella blinked as the question took her by surprise.

"Are you insane?" her voice squeaked in shock.

"Most likely," he growled. "Make me crazier. It's your chance for revenge, Ella. Tell me how wet your pussy is."

She bit her lip, breathing fast and hard as she seriously considered the request.

"Go back to work," she finally whispered desperately, shaking her head.

"Ella, remember how nice I was to you yesterday when my mouth sucked that sweet little clit of yours?"

How could she forget?

"I didn't ask you to break into my room, James."

"I want you to suck my cock like that, Ella. While you're tied belly down on my bed, my cock thrusting slow and easy in your mouth and I inflate the plug I'm going to push up your sweet, virgin ass."

"Stop. Why are you doing this to me?" Her pussy was gushing between her thighs, so hot it felt blistered by her need. "For God's sake, James, surely you can find someone to fuck. Do you have to torture me this way?"

She pushed her fingers through her loose hair, feeling the silky strands brush her shoulders, almost shivering at the caress against her ultra sensitive flesh. She was being driven crazy, and he knew it. Maybe it was some kind of messed up mid-life crisis, she thought desperately. Because she knew her own arousal had never tormented her to this degree. It was hell and she wanted it to stop. She wanted him to leave. Or did she?

"I won't waste my breath answering that question," he bit out as he stooped down at the end of the lounger. "You want to control it, Ella? Do you really think you can?"

He was so handsome he broke her heart. Hard and toned, his body muscular and so filled with male grace that it took her breath every time she looked at him. And his face, arrogant with just a touch of the aristocratic in his strong, straight nose and superior expression.

"James, I'm asking you to stop this." Her heart was racing out of control. How was she supposed to deny him when her body ached so desperately for him?

He was like a fever in her blood. As long as she stayed away from him, she could survive it. But now, with his desire for her so clear, her needs raging through her body, she couldn't find the will to resist him. She was weak. She admitted it and she hated it. Hated the emotional and physical responses that she couldn't fight any longer.

"Lay back for me, Ella," he whispered softly. "Lay back, and let me show you what I can do for you."

Ella watched him helplessly. Her body was tense, demanding action. Demanding that she do as he ask and lay back in the lounger for him. She watched as his tongue touched his sensual lips, as though anticipating a meal, and she knew what he wanted. Knew what he would do to her. Her pussy gushed in response.

She whimpered as he moved, his hands reaching for her arms, pulling them gently, taking the support she used to keep her body upright as he released the back support of the lounger. He lowered her until her back rested on the flat surface.

Ella stared up at him, trembling, hating the weakness that flooded her body. Damn him. He was so assured, so sensual, so damned tempting she could barely keep her senses intact.

"James." Her breath caught in arousal as his fingers went to the tiny buttons of her bodice. Her breasts were unbound beneath the fabric, her nipples hard, on fire for his touch.

"I've dreamed of touching you, Ella," he whispered, his green eyes darkening, the thick black lashes lowering sensually over the wicked orbs. "Ached to taste you. Do you have any idea the hell I've gone through for the last ten years, wanting to hear you scream my name as you climax for me?"

A whimper escaped her lips as the last button of the dress came free, and he was able to spread the edges apart with slow deliberation. Her body was laid out before him then, only the thin silk of her panties left to cover the front of her body.

"You're wet for me, Ella," he whispered, his eyes centering on the pale green triangle of fabric. "And you still shave your pretty pussy, don't you? When my tongue caresses it, laps up all that thick cream, you'll feel every soft touch, won't you?"

His hand spread her legs slowly. Ella gripped the sides of the lounger, watching him, mesmerized by the sensuality in his expression, the hunger reflected in his eyes, in the curve of his lips.

"James." She whispered his name, her voice rough, pleading as she caught his hands when they moved to the band of her panties. "I can't..." She couldn't finish the sentence, couldn't force the words past her lips.

"Can't what, baby?" he asked her gently, his fingers hooking in the elastic, pulling her panties down, away from her weak grip. "Can't lay back and feel good for me? Can't see if what we've waited for all these years isn't as good as our imaginations? Why can't you do that?"

He was hypnotizing her, she thought desperately. Stealing her will with the sound of his deep, rough voice. Making her crazy for him with that dark, hooded look.

She trembled as he removed the scrap of silk then spread her legs wider. All the while he watched her from the side of the lounger, his chest moving hard and fast, as he seemed to fight for breath himself, his eyes darkening lustfully.

"Damn, Ella, you're prettier than I ever imagined." His hand moved up her thigh until his fingers grazed the desperate heat and thick juices that coated her cunt. The proof of her weakness. The proof that she was just as depraved, just as perverted as Jase had been, because she knew, knew beyond a shadow of a doubt, exactly what James wanted from her.

"I can't." She jerked from him, moving before he could stop her, stumbling from the lounger then rushing desperately away from him. Away from her own needs.

Chapter Seven

ꟹ

Jumping to her feet, she rushed to her bedroom, fighting her tears, her fears. James' voice was dark, angry behind her, spurring her forward, making her heart beat in dread. If he touched her again, asked her again, she wouldn't be able to refuse him. He was her weakness. He was her sin.

She slammed the door behind her then fought to drag the suitcase from her closet. She couldn't stand it. If he wouldn't leave, then she would. He could have the fucking house. Do whatever the hell he wanted. She couldn't stand it anymore. She ignored her dress as it flared away from the front of her body, ignored her nakedness beneath it. She had to leave, had to get away from him.

Bent over, her mind centered on pulling the damned case from the small utility closet, she was unaware that James had followed her until he burst into the bedroom, gripped her hips and tossed her on the bed.

"Damn you," she screeched as she came to her knees, clutching the sides of her dress. Her eyes widened as she watched him undress. Slowly. Watching her with narrowed, intent eyes.

The air in the bedroom heated, thinned, until she had to fight for breath. She sat on her knees, gripping the edges of her dress together, fighting just to breathe as each article of clothing was dropped to the floor, until he wore nothing but his own brazen sexuality.

Dear God. He was naked. All dark, sleek skin and toned muscle. Especially the bulging length of his cock. It was thick and hard, the head flared and appearing bruised, it was so engorged with blood. She couldn't take her eyes from it, couldn't stop the whimper that escaped her lips.

"First lesson," he growled dominantly, his voice brooking no refusal. "Take your dress off and lay down on the bed."

"Are you insane?" She repeated her earlier question.

"Most likely," he bit out, his hand going to the engorged flesh rising between his thighs. She watched, mesmerized, as his fingers stroked the hard cock. "So it might be best to placate me."

She licked her lips. "What are you going to do?"

He walked over to the dresser and picked up the articles she hadn't seen until then, in one hand. He must have placed them there before coming to her on the back porch.

The first looked like a slender cock, the middle thinner than the flared head, with a hose and bulb leading from the base. With it was a small tube of gel lubrication. In the other hand, he picked up the leather wrist and ankle restraints. Her eyes widened.

"I'm going to fuck your ass, eventually," he told her softly. "While I'm fucking your sweet mouth and your tight little pussy, I'm going to be preparing your ass to take me. The inflatable plug will take care of that. "

Inflatable? How much did it inflate? It already looked too damned big to her.

"James, please." She shook her head, reduced to pleading. "Don't do this to me. I don't think I can bear it." Physically she was dying for it; emotionally, she was terrified.

"We'll start out easy." He wasn't asking her, he was demanding. "Undress and lie on the bed."

"Why?" She couldn't take her eyes off the restraints. "Why do you have to tie me down?"

He laid everything at the bottom of the bed. "It's all about control." He eased the straps of her sundress from her shoulders. "The one losing it, the one possessing it. My pleasure, Ella, comes from yours. But you think you have to control that pleasure. Fight it. I want you restrained, unable to run from me, unable to fight what I need to give you. I want you to lose that control that keeps you locked inside your own fears." She trembled as the material of her dress skimmed her swollen breasts.

"I don't like it," she whispered, almost groaning as his lips feathered her shoulder.

"If your pussy doesn't get wet and hot for me, if your body doesn't scream out for more, then I'll stop. I'll know if it's not right for you." The dress fell to the bed behind her. "Now, lie down for me, on your stomach first."

Ella licked her lips. God she wanted him. She had controlled it with Jase, no matter the fantasies of James that had tormented her. Surely she could control her heart, if nothing else.

Shaken, weakened by her own desires, her own fantasies, she did as he ordered.

"Have you ever been taken anally, Ella?" he asked her then. "Not a plug, but by Jase, or anyone else?"

She shook her head, careful to keep her face buried in the blankets of the bed. He attached the leather restraints to her legs first, the small links of the chains rattling as he secured them to the short bedposts. He moved then to her wrists. His hands were gentle, caressing, the leather cool as he secured it above each hand before securing the chains to the headboard.

She was spread out. Though there was some slack in the chains, she wouldn't be able to go far if she did move. She shuddered, dragging in air with a sense of desperation as her arousal intensified. Never with Jase had she felt the trepidation and searing desire that she did now. As though she had known Jase was no threat to her, neither emotionally nor sexually, but James was. He could destroy her. If she let him.

"So nice," he whispered as he moved back to the bottom of the bed, moving between her spread thighs.

His hands ran up the backs of her thighs as she trembled beneath his touch. Long-fingered and broad, his hands were warm and slightly calloused, creating an exciting friction on her flesh.

"I used to hide and watch you whenever I saw you out in public," he whispered. "I knew you would run if you saw me, and I loved watching you move, Ella. Watching the sweet curves of your ass flex, the line of your back, the tilt of your head. I would drink the sight of you in."

Ella's hands clenched in the blankets beneath her as his hands cupped the lower curves of her rear, spreading her apart sensually. She could feel her cunt, drenched and hot, rippling with convulsive shudders of need. She couldn't stop the involuntary flexing of her buttocks, or the little whimper that escaped her throat.

"Are you comfortable?" he asked her, his voice low, rough.

"No." She had to fight for air. She felt intoxicated and yet on the edge of panic.

"Good." He patted her rear a little sharply in approval. Ella flinched at the tingling heat that washed up her spine from the light tap. "Now, I want you to try to relax for me a little, Ella. I want to put the plug inside you, get you ready, before we go any further."

Relax? He was kidding, she thought. He had to be.

She felt him moving at the bottom of the bed, his body shifting beneath her before his hair brushed her leg. She jerked as his hands went under her thighs, lifting her a bit before his tongue thrust hard and fast inside the soaked channel of her pussy.

"Oh God! James!" she cried out, her back bowing in reflex, angling her hips higher for the invasion.

His tongue was like a flame, searing her vagina as he pushed in hard, then pulled back slowly. As though he had already shaken the foundations of her desire, he began to lap at her. His tongue licked and stroked, drawing her juices from her body as he murmured his appreciation of her taste, or her need, she wasn't certain.

His fingers moved to the gentle curve of her cunt lips, spreading them marginally as his tongue delved lower, licking through the slit, circling her clit. Teasing strokes of his demon tongue had her grinding her pussy into his mouth, and yet with little ease. As she moved closer, his mouth drew farther away.

She was only barely aware of his fingers probing between her buttocks, slick with the cool gel of the lubrication that coated them. One long finger pierced her puckered opening as James' tongue speared deep inside her cunt once again.

Ella's eyes flew open as a gasp escaped her lips. Braced only partially on her knees, the slack in the restraints taken up by her position, there was no way to escape the invasion. She moaned, a drawn out sound of shocked pleasure, heated pain as his tongue fucked her clenching vagina once again.

"James," she whimpered his name, fighting to hold onto her control.

Her anus stretched around the probing finger, welcoming the heated sensations that came from his smooth, stroking movements. He didn't answer her unspoken plea, one she wasn't certain of herself, rather he pulled the finger back, added another and pushed into the tight entrance once again.

A cry strangled in Ella's throat.

"Easy, darlin'." His voice was a rough croon as his fingers began to gently scissor inside her anus, stretching her slowly as he slurped at the juices running from her heated cunt.

The bite of pain was intoxicating, addicting. Pleasure swelled inside her as he stretched her, licked her, his other hand moving up her body until it tucked beneath her breast, his fingers plucking at her nipple. She was shaking, suspended between lust and that sharp bite of pain, and terrified he would stop.

He prepared her slowly. The pleasure became a tormenting surge of sensations as his fingers prepared her anus gently. There was no impatience, as Jase had often shown, no irritation that it took so long to prepare her. Beneath his unhurried caresses she eased, relaxed, until he was working three long fingers in and out of the back passage as her strangled moans echoed around the room.

"Yes, baby," he crooned into the dripping folds of her pussy. "So sweet and tight, Ella."

She moaned in protest as his fingers pulled free, then moaned again in rising pleasure as his tongue began circling her clit. She was unaware of his hands for long moments, unaware that more was coming. Her dazed senses only knew his hard breaths between her thighs, his stroking tongue…

Chapter Eight

ꕥ

"James..." She wailed his name as the head of the butt plug seared her anus as he pushed it into the tight entrance.

She fought the restraints, pressed harder into his licking tongue and nearly came to the smooth, stroking movements as fire lanced through her rectum. Thickly lubricated, the plug invaded her slowly, stretching her, burning her, bringing her so close to orgasm she had to bite her lip to keep from screaming out for it.

"James, please." She couldn't stop the strangled plea tearing from her throat as the anal plug lodged inside her anus, her muscles clenching on it, her pussy shuddering in reaction to the pleasure/pain.

He moved then, despite her protesting cry, pulling himself from beneath her thighs and kneeling behind her. Her hips arched to him, her body desperate, mindless. His hand landed on the upturned cheek of her ass in a surprisingly sharp blow.

Ella stilled. At first, shock arced through her body, then an excitement that had her stilling in fear. She didn't like it, she assured herself. It was depraved, perverted. She wouldn't like it.

"From now on, if you need to get off, Ella, you come to me. No more vibrators unless I insert them. Do you understand me?"

"James..." She shook her head, needing to protest, yet unable to.

His hand landed on the opposite cheek of her ass. She flinched, her body shuddering at the heat. She wouldn't like this, she promised herself, though her pussy convulsed in nearing orgasm.

Then she felt the plug, seated so snugly in her rear, begin to swell. Slowly stretching her, burning her as his fingers went to her dripping vagina. One slid slowly inside her, caressing the thin muscle that separated her vagina from her anus. She could feel the enlargement of the plug as he caressed her there. The steady growth, the burning pain, the striking pleasure that shot through her body like flares of lightning.

"The plug enlarges, Ella, to eight and a half inches and several inches around. Almost as thick, almost as long, as my cock." She was struggling for breath when the swelling stopped. "Seven inches is all you can take now. When you can take it all, Ella, then I'll fuck you there."

Ella writhed against the blankets, fighting to accept the thickness of the device that stretched her anus. She could feel the heat steaming from her pussy, the sensitivity of her body, the agonizing need that was as much pain as it was pleasure.

"Here, baby." He was beside her then. Ella opened her eyes, staring up at him as he helped her to lever herself up as far as the chains he had loosened would allow.

She trembled, knowing what he wanted, more than eager to give it to him. She licked her lips slowly then allowed his cock to push slowly between them. He was thick and hard, so hot and demanding she moaned in exquisite anticipation as she closed her lips tightly around him and suckled slowly at his flesh. He burrowed in, sliding over her tongue until he was almost gagging her, poised at the entrance to her throat.

He stopped, breathing roughly as his hand wrapped around the flesh where her lips were closed around it. Then his hips began to move. She heard his groan as her tongue licked at him, her mouth sucking him as he began to fuck her with smooth, powerful strokes. She was restrained, at his mercy, a receptacle for whatever he commanded. She was helpless. She was insane with lust.

She suckled his cock with moist, noisy appreciation. There was no shame in the sounds she made, no trepidation that he would give her more than she could take. At least, not in this instance. There was only the hot male taste of him. Only the need to make him as crazy to come as she was.

"Damn, even your mouth is tight," he groaned as he fucked her slowly. "Hot and tight, Ella. But your pussy's going to be hotter, tighter. Like fucking a virgin with that butt plug filling your ass, tightening your cunt."

She trembled as his wicked words washed over her, but she suckled his cock like a woman starved for a man. She licked beneath the head, slurped at it, starved for the taste of his seed. The shaft throbbed, pulsed, but he held onto his control as she slowly lost hers.

"Enough," he growled long moments later as he pulled back from her.

Ella moaned in protest, struggling against the restraints, as she tried to follow the burgeoning erection. His hand landed on the curve of her ass again. A warning slap that only made her pussy vibrate with increased need.

"I've got to fuck you, Ella. I'll strangle you if I try to take my pleasure in your mouth now."

Ella stilled. Her breath rasped from her throat, fear suddenly trembling through her with almost the same force as her lust did. His cock was large, thick. The plug in her anus had tightened her vagina, and it had been more than a decade since anything larger than her small vibrator had invaded the channel. He would kill her with his cock…

"Not like this, I want to watch you take me, Ella." She was too weak to fight him as he released the restraints on her ankles and her wrists.

He turned her over on her back then replaced them carefully. Ella stared up at him, unable to protest, unable to fight him. She ached in ways she could have never imagined. Her pussy felt as though it was boiling with heat, and the fullness in her anus only called attention to the emptiness of her vagina.

He leaned over her, his expression so gentle, so filled with approval that her heart clenched. When his lips covered hers, her womb flexed with melting desire. His kiss was hot, heated, tasting of her intimate juices and his male need. She moaned into his lips, wishing she could hold him to her, touch him, as she felt his cock nudge against the sensitive opening of her vagina.

"Ella," he groaned her name, his hand touching her damp hair, the other holding her hip as the head of his cock invaded her tight opening.

"Oh God! James!" Her head tossed as he began to push slowly inside.

"Easy, Ella. It's okay, baby. You can take me." She struggled against the restraints, crying out as he separated the sensitive muscles, powering through the drenched, fisted grip of her pussy.

She bucked beneath him, barely aware of her sharp cries of pleasure…or were they of pain? Her movements drove him deeper inside her. Deeper. Deeper. Her hips arched to him as he slid in to the hilt, the pulse and throb of the heavy veins beneath his hard flesh echoing through her body.

"Damn you, Ella," he cursed her, his voice rough as he fought for control. "You're so fucking tight I could come now. Look what you've denied us all these years. All these years, Ella, you stole this from us."

She screamed then. She had sworn she would never scream for him. But when he began the hard driving rhythm inside her tight clasp, the pleasure/pain that tore through her body pushed the desperate scream from her throat. She was bound to the bed, unable to fight the sensations, helpless against the rocking strokes that tore past her muscles, made her accept her own desires, the pain and the pleasure and the need for more.

Too many years longing. Too many nights dreaming. On the third stroke Ella exploded. The orgasm that tore through her body had her tightening further, screaming out his name, her body shaking, tensing, convulsing as she fought the strength of her release. But she couldn't fight it. Couldn't escape the hard, quickening strokes of his cock as he fucked her through the cataclysm, then a last desperate lunge as his seed jetted hot and harsh inside her convulsing pussy.

"Ella." He cried out her name as his lips buried at her neck.

She felt his release spurting inside her, her own rushing through her quaking vagina as her soul rocked with the pleasure, and she knew the emotions she had fought for so many years.

Her vision dimmed as she lost her breath with the last wave of intense sensation. Tears fell from her eyes, and as she collapsed back on the bed, she knew in her soul she would never be the same again.

Chapter Nine

ꟈ

"Hey, Ella, you missed dinner. Are you in there?" Ella jerked awake at the sound of her friend's voice that evening, her shocked eyes going to the bedside clock. Damn, she had forgotten about Charlie having the key to the house, and her habit of just coming in as she pleased.

It was dark, a little after ten, and James was still in the bed with her. Even worse, his half erect cock was still buried in her pussy where it had been after her last climax.

She moved to jerk away, but his arm around her hips stopped her, and her heart raced as his cock began to harden inside her.

"In a minute, Charlie," she called out, pushing at his arm. "I fell asleep. I'm sorry. I'll be out in a minute."

"Well, hurry," Charlie called back. "It's getting late and I need to head home."

The sound of the other woman's footsteps fading away from the bedroom door eased her harsh breathing until she felt James thrust inside the tight grip of her vagina as his throttled groan sounded at her ear.

"I have to get up," she whispered, pulling at his arm, wanting nothing better than to push back against him, to scream out in the pleasure again.

"Damn," he muttered, though there was no anger in his tone, only regret.

Ella bit her lip as the hot length of flesh eased from her and he rolled lazily to his back as he reached over and flipped on the light at his side of the bed. She looked back at him as she wrapped the blanket around her and rose to her feet. He was naked and unashamed of it. His long fingers scratched at his chest as he smothered a drowsy yawn. His erection lay against his lower stomach, glistening with her juices and his earlier release. He looked sexy as hell.

Ella shook her head before he could tempt her any further, grabbed her robe and rushed to the bathroom. It took longer than she would have liked to clean the evidence of their spent passion from her body. Thankfully, James had removed the butt plug earlier, though her vagina, and her tender back entrance were still a little sensitive.

Ten minutes later, she left the bathroom, covered in her long gown and robe. James still lay on the bed, watching her through narrowed eyes.

"She doesn't know you're here," she whispered.

His eyes narrowed further. "Who does know?"

She licked her lips nervously. "Just Tess and Cole."

"I see." His tone of voice suggested he might see more than she was actually saying. "So you want me to stay put?"

She shrugged. Hell yes, she did. Her friends rarely kept secrets. What Charlie knew, Terrie would know, and Marey would know and Tamera. She winced at the thought. She especially didn't want Tamera to know.

"Fine." He shrugged, though she didn't trust his tone of voice. "Go visit your friend. I'll be here when you're done."

He closed his eyes. Ella breathed in deeply in relief before she rushed from the room.

* * * * *

"It's about time. What were you doing in there, anyway?" Charlie turned from the refrigerator as Ella moved into the kitchen.

Charlie was nearly five years younger than Ella, slim and sophisticated, dressed in a gray silk sheath with matching heels. Her long, black hair fell to the middle of her shoulders like a fall of midnight silk, contrasting to the perfect peaches and cream perfection of her bare shoulders.

"I was asleep." Ella went to the coffee pot and put on a fresh brew of coffee.

"You're never asleep before midnight, Ella," Charlie scoffed. "Hell, you're still up at one and two in the morning. I know, I can see your bedroom light from my house."

Ella lowered her head. She was unaware Charlie kept such a close eye on her. It was disconcerting.

"Sometimes I take a nap." She shrugged, flipping the switch and listening to the machine begin to hum as it began to heat the water. "It's no big deal."

She turned back to her friend, aware of Charlie's steady regard as she took a slice of cheesecake from the refrigerator and moved to the table. She collected a fork from the cabinet as she passed by it, but still, she watched Ella.

"What's going on? You're acting strange." Charlie was the most perceptive of her friends, but Ella didn't like how easily even she was reading her.

"Nothing's going on." Ella moved two cups from the cabinet and set cream and sugar on the table. "I was just tired, Charlie."

She was just damned uncomfortable now. Her thighs were weak and tender, her breasts marked by James' mouth, her body longing to return to him. She usually enjoyed her friend's visits and looked forward to them. Charlie was usually easy going and filled with laughter, but now she just wanted her to leave. Ella wanted to return to James, his heat, his hard body.

"Ella, you aren't acting right, honey." Charlie watched her with sharp, deep blue eyes. "What's going on?"

"Nothing." Ella shook her head as she poured the coffee. She had to fight the trembling of her hands, and the knowledge that everything was suddenly out of control. And not just sexually.

She set Charlie's coffee cup in front of her, then moved to the other side of the table and sat down. As she looked up, her stomach dropped. Charlie was staring across the room in complete shock. Ella's head turned slowly, knowing what held her rapt attention. Her brows snapped into a frown as James walked barefoot through the kitchen.

"You didn't tell me you were fixing coffee, baby." He wore blue jeans and nothing else. And those damned jeans. The top button was loose, and the waistband rode low on his tight abdomen. Right above it was a strawberry love bite. She remembered marking him, and now her face flamed as she realized her friend couldn't miss it.

"Dear God," Charlie breathed as she obviously fought for breath, her gaze swinging from Ella to James.

Ella could only cover her face as James poured his coffee, dropped a quick kiss to the top of her head and said, "I'll finish up some of that paperwork you dragged me away from earlier while you talk to your friend."

She peeked through her fingers as he ambled away. The jeans molded his buttocks to perfection, and Charlie wasn't missing a second of the view as he left the room.

As he disappeared through the doorway, Charlie turned to her, her eyes wide, her expression shocked.

"James Wyman," she breathed out in shock. "Oh my God! Ella, you fucked James Wyman? Or is it Jesse?" she squeaked in fear, well aware of Tess's interlude with Jesse Wyman and Cole.

Ella squirmed in her chair. No, she thought, he had fucked her, thoroughly. And more than once. She sighed tiredly. Everyone would know it now.

"It's not Jesse," she groaned, pushing her fingers restlessly through her hair. "You should know better than that."

"James!" she squealed.

"Dammit, Charlie, shut up," she shushed her frantically. "He'll hear you."

"Ella, do you have any idea what you're doing? What you're getting into?" Her voice lowered. "Honey, he and Jesse have shared their women more than once…"

"Not me." Ella came out of her chair, her hands trembling violently as she shoved them into the pockets of her robe.

"Maybe not with Jesse, but Ella, James and Jesse aren't the only members of their pack, hon. I could name you half a dozen now."

She shook her head. "What the hell are you talking about?"

Charlie sat back in her chair, her mouth falling open in surprise. "You haven't heard? They're called the Trojans, babe. Because of their dominance, and their sharing. They like submissives, Ella. You aren't a submissive. Are you?"

"You know I'm not," Ella bit out. But she wondered. What James had done to her that night, the dark promises he had made to her as he buried his cock inside her over and over again, threatened her belief that she wasn't.

"Ella, those men, they don't mess with women who aren't submissive. Women who won't give them that ultimate commitment." Charlie came to her feet, facing her in concern. "You ran from Jase because of his demands. James will be worse."

Ella shook her head. "I'm in control," she whispered. "He won't do it if I don't want it."

"And when he leaves because you can't do it?" she whispered fiercely. "Dammit, Ella, haven't you been hurt enough?"

"It's my choice, Charlie." She raised her head in determination. "My choice. No matter what happens."

Charlie watched her silently.

"He's the one," she finally said slowly. "The one that came in while Jase had you tied down. The reason you divorced him and moved so damned far away for so long."

Ella turned away, her lips opening as she fought to drag in more air, to stem the panic rising in her chest.

"Stop, Charlie," she whispered, turning back to her as she stared at her friend pleadingly. "Please, let it go."

"My God. You're in love with him." Charlie shook her head, amazement shaping her expression. "Ella, he's the one. The reason you ran and turned into a bitter old nun. My God. He's younger than you are."

"Six years..."

"He shares his women," she pointed out again.

"I don't have to agree..."

"But you will to keep him." Charlie was angry now. Her voice throbbed with it, her face flushing with it. "You will, Ella. Because you love him."

"Enough." Her hand sliced through the air as her soul trembled with the knowledge. "This isn't any of your business, Charlie..."

"The hell it isn't." Charlie's voice rose with her anger. "Dammit, Ella, I watched you destroy yourself after that divorce. Turning into a bitter old woman before your time because of that bastard..."

"Lower your voice." Ella was shaking with her own anger now. "And remember, Charlie, I didn't ask you for your opinion then or now."

"Like you have to ask for it," Charlie snorted in disgust. "Really, Ella. It's voluntary, darling." The sarcasm was a clear sign that Charlie was rapidly losing her temper. Ella wasn't far behind.

"Everything okay?" Ella's head swung around to the doorway and she wanted to groan in dismay when she saw James standing there, watching them mockingly.

"Don't you know how to dress?" she bit out in irritation, seeing all the smooth, perfect muscle that she knew Charlie was eating up with her eyes.

He arched a dark brow questioningly. "I thought all good little boy toys went around half-naked? Don't tell me you're firing me after only a few hours on the job."

Chapter Ten

ঌ

It was well after midnight before Charlie left. After James's mocking statement and his declaration that he was going to bed to let them discuss him in peace, Ella broke out the wine. Some nights, there was nothing you could do but get a shade tipsy and remember all the reasons why you didn't want a man in your life. Charlie was eager to go along with her. Evidently all that smooth male muscle and blatant sexuality had been too much for her to deal with at one time as well.

Finally, her friend weaved her way to the limo waiting on her, thanked her aging driver nicely as he opened the door for her, and crawled into the vehicle. Ella herself felt she was walking reasonably straight until she closed the door and turned around. She proceeded to walk into the embroidered chair that sat off to the side. She frowned down at it in irritation before backing up and trying again.

She needed to go to bed. But James was in her bed. She stopped as she headed through the kitchen. Of course James was in her bed. That was where he belonged, she decided with a sharp, rather jerky nod before squaring her shoulders and heading to the room.

He was waiting on her. How had she known he would still be awake and waiting on her? His expression was cool, arrogant, as she removed her robe and started to lie down.

"The gown." His voice was dark, foreboding.

Ella stopped, staring at him in surprise.

"Excuse me?" she asked him haughtily. "I sleep in my gown."

"Take it off or I'll tear it off." There was no mercy in his voice, no change in his expression.

Ella snorted. "Some boy toy you are, James. I might have to fire you after all. You are supposed to obey me, not the other way around."

"Take the gown off. I won't tell you again, Ella." Her insides trembled at the dark brew of anger and desire that throbbed in his voice.

She did as he said, suddenly too nervous not to. She watched him helplessly as the silk gown slithered to the floor, leaving her bare before his eyes. What did he see, she wondered? She was older; her body wasn't as toned, as pretty as it had been ten years before. She knew all her problem areas, had stared at them in the mirror more times than she could count.

He pulled the blankets back then and patted the bed beside him. Watching him warily, she got into bed, lying on her back as he stopped her from turning on her side. His big hand moved to her stomach, caressing the flesh there as her breath caught in her throat.

"I won't be relegated to the bedroom, hidden, a secret you keep from everyone," he warned her coldly as he stared down at her. "Do you understand me, Ella?"

"What do you want from me?" She shook her head, her brain clouded with the alcohol, her emotions sensitized from her friend's warnings, and James's demands. "Why are you even here, James? In my bed. My life," she sighed wearily.

"You have to figure that one out on your own," he growled, his hand moving until he could brush back the lingering strands of hair that clung to her cheek, her neck. "You should have already figured it out, Ella, but you refuse to look beyond your own fears. I won't allow that to continue."

His eyes softened only marginally as she stared up at him. In the soft light of the lamp, his features were shadowed, savage yet softening with tenderness. She lifted her hand until she could touch the roughness of his beard-shadowed jaw, loving the warmth and roughness of his flesh.

"I dreamed of you," she whispered bleakly. "For so many years, I dreamed of you, James. You'll break my heart if I let you. I can't let you."

His gaze became shuttered. "Go to sleep, Ella. We'll talk tomorrow."

He moved then, turning out the light before lying down beside her, wrapping his arms around her as he pulled her close. Ella stared up at the dark ceiling, feeling the warmth and vitality of his body as he held her. Feeling the hard length of his cock against her thigh.

She breathed out regretfully. "I'll miss you when you're gone, James."

"Go to sleep, Ella," he warned, his voice soft yet commanding. "You don't want to push me much further tonight."

"But I will, James." She shook her head, the wistful sadness inside her heart too much to bear. "I was used to being alone."

Silence met her words. He wasn't asleep; his body was too tight, too tense for her to believe that. His anger thickened the air in the room, though, and she realized she didn't really want him angry. Keeping him angry was to keep him at arm's length, a safe distance from making her body torment her with its needs. But he was close now, he had already taken her, more than once, and the little aches in her body proved that.

"I used to fantasize about you." She frowned as she thought of the years that had passed. "How silly is that, James? That's when what little satisfaction I had found with Jase in all those years was gone. The moment you stepped into that room destroyed it all."

His cock jerked against her thigh.

"I warned you, Ella. I won't warn you again." She shivered at the dominating tone of his voice.

She turned her head to look at him, seeing only the shadowed impression of his form beside her. Her eyes lowered as she wondered what it would be like to see him out of control. All that cool purpose burned away. Could she do it? Could she make James Wyman, master of women, lose control? Her pussy gushed with the thought. She had heard rumors for years. Women talked, and unfortunately she heard the tales. And they talked about James and his cool control, his sexual deliberation. None had broken that calm. None had made him lose control.

She rolled on her side slowly, shivering as she felt him adjust his erection to her new position. His body tightened further.

"Maybe having a boy toy would be nice." She smoothed her hand up his chest, her nails glancing his hard male nipple as she scratched lightly over it.

He caught her hand, holding it still against his chest as he stared at her through the darkness.

"Do you think I'd make a good toy, Ella?" he asked her, his voice silky, dangerous. "It could blow up in your hands, sweetheart. You don't want to continue on the course."

She was just tipsy enough to smile. To lean forward and swirl her tongue over the sensitive nub of his nipple. She heard his breath catch, felt his body tighten further.

"Isn't that the point?" she asked him as she moved lower, her tongue stroking down his hard abdomen as the muscles there clenched tightly.

His hands threaded through her hair, clenching on the strands as she nipped at his flesh, trying to halt her movements. Ella couldn't halt her gasp. The prickling heat in her scalp was more exciting then she wanted to admit.

"Ella." He spoke her name sharply, a demand, a command to stop, warning her in the sheer dangerous throb that lingered in the tone.

"What, James?" she asked him softly. Her head held still just below his heart, but her hands were free. She raked her nails up his thighs, loving the sound of his breath catching in his throat.

"You don't want me to lose control, Ella," he warned her softly.

"Of course I don't," she whispered, her teeth nipping at his skin as her nails ran alongside his bulging cock.

It was exhilarating, exciting. He was breathing harder now, his heart racing beneath her ear. She tugged at the grip on her hair, whimpering with the stimulation, that sharp flare of pleasure that raced through her body. Her head lowered until her tongue was able to reach the flared, hot crown of his cock. He jerked as she licked it.

The grip he had on her hair was fierce, the burning along her scalp intense, but it only fired her body as a distant amazement pierced her brain. The pain was a fiery cascade of sensations that nearly broke her. She was out of control. She, who had kept her control wrapped about her like a mantle of protection, had fallen as easily to this man as a virgin with no knowledge of the heartache awaiting her.

She pulled further against his grip, crying out as she felt her cunt clench at the ache. Her lips capped the turgid head of his erection, slurping noisily as her tongue licked, stroked. She wanted him deep within her mouth, wanted to feel him fucking into it, unable to halt his own spiraling pleasure. To destroy his control as he had destroyed hers.

One hand gripped the thick shaft as his hips jerked, burying the smooth crown in her suckling mouth. She heard his strangled moan above her, felt his erection throb with a deep, hard flex of the tightened muscle.

"Enough." His voice was thicker now as he pulled at her hair. When that didn't help, he gripped her head, pulling her up as she cried in protest.

He flipped her to her back, jerking the blankets off the bed as he came over her.

"You don't want this, Ella," he bit out fiercely. "You don't want to tempt me this way."

She undulated beneath him, raking her hard-tipped breasts against his chest, rubbing her aching pussy against the thigh wedged between her legs.

"What will you do, James?" she asked him, tempting him, tempting fate and the dark visions suddenly rushing through her head. "How will you punish me? Will you share me then, to show me my place? To regain your control?"

He stilled. His hands held her wrists to the mattress as he stared down at her, his savage expression only barely discernable. He was breathing hard and fast now, fighting to regain the upper hand, and now she knew how to make him lose it.

"Can you bear it, James?" she asked him softly. "Will you join in, or merely watch as another man takes me, making me scream as you do, fucking me like you do…"

Before she could anticipate him, his control broke. His legs wedged between her thighs and his cock pushed inside her swollen pussy in one hard, long stroke. She screamed out at the invasion, at the instant, fiery pleasure.

"Do you know what you're tempting, Ella?" he groaned as she fought to accept the heavy girth buried in her cunt. "Do you know what you're doing to me?"

He wasn't still. His hips moved, his cock thrusting in and out of her in long smooth strokes as he fought to hold back. She didn't want him to hold back. *She* didn't want to hold back. Not any longer.

"How will you do it, James? How can you make me accept it? I dare you to try."

She didn't expect the consequences of those words. His lips slammed down on hers, slanting across hers as his tongue drove deep into her mouth. At the same time, the thrusts of his cock inside her vagina increased in strength and power.

Ella cried into the kiss, her tongue tangling with his as she tilted her hips to take him deeper, harder inside her sensitive cunt. She could feel her muscles gripping him, the thickness, the heat of his erection thrusting past the sensitive tissue, stroking nerve endings already enflamed with a lust she had never thought herself capable of.

And with each stroke, each demanding invasion into the core of her body, she was reminded of what caused his loss of control. The thought of her with him and with another. Two cocks, hard and strong, pushing into her over and over again…

Her body tightened, her cunt clamping down on the pistoning power of his cock as she exploded to the images twisting through her mind, her body. She tried to scream, but her mouth with filled with James. She tried to buck him away from her, to escape the driving pleasure, the knowledge, but her pussy was filled with James. Filled with him until he groaned hard and deep, powered into her one last brutal thrust before he exploded.

The wash of his hot seed inside her channel triggered another, smaller climax as she whimpered beneath him. Her body shuddered, her womb rippling with the orgasm as the ice that had once encased her heart shattered.

She loved James Wyman. And Ella knew to the farthest depths of her soul, that the love filling her would be her ultimate destruction.

Chapter Eleven

"I'll be back in three hours." Ella lay face down on the bed at noon the next day, breathing through the fiery fullness that invaded her anus.

James had taken her again when they woke up. He had been quiet, almost reflective as they showered and ate breakfast. Later they had lain around the pool until after a light lunch that he had prepared himself. They hadn't talked much, but the silence hadn't been uncomfortable.

Ella had been wary, though. He wasn't pushing her, for anything. He was contemplative as though his loss of control the night before bothered him in some way. An hour after lunch he laid out the box that contained a mild anal douche and ordered her to use it. His voice had hardened, sending heat streaking through her pussy.

"So what am I supposed to do for three hours?" She turned her head, watching him with narrowed eyes.

Preparing her for the anal invasion had left her hot, wet. She wanted him now, before he left.

"Wait on me." His voice brooked no refusal. "Leave the plug in. I've removed the inflator, so you can dress, do what you normally do. Just do it as it eases the muscles there."

He had inflated it farther than before. Through a tormenting hour of heated touches, burning strokes of his tongue in and out of her pussy, but never enough to push her over the edge. She was burning with lust now and reluctant to move. The thick intruder buried in her anus stretched the muscles there with fiery precision. He had given her all she could take, yet had assured her that it still had not been fully inflated.

"Oh, that's fair..." She stopped. The look in his eyes was almost frightening.

She settled back on the bed, watching as his brooding look eased only slightly.

"You pushed last night, Ella. You may think you've gotten away with it, but you haven't. When I get back, I'll show you just how you haven't. If you get yourself off, I'll punish you, Ella. I'll tie you down to this bed and leave you there for the remainder of the night, and I'll make sure you know how painful arousal can really be."

She trembled at the sound of his voice. She had no doubt he would do it, too. If she was restrained, there would be no tempting his control, no pushing his personal limits. He could torment her as long as he liked. He had proved that in the last hour.

He released the restraints that held her, leaving the chains attached to the bed as he moved away from her.

"Wear a dress. Something loose and light. When I get back, we'll see how much control you have, baby."

Something about those words had trepidation skittering through her body. She eased up slowly on the bed, feeling her pussy clench, drench further as the plug bit at her tender anal muscles. She stared up at him silently, watching as his eyes darkened, his body tensing at the sight of her swollen, hard-tipped breasts, and the arousal that she knew was obvious in her expression.

"What are you going to do, James?" she asked him softly.

"You know, Ella." He pushed his hands into the pockets of his slacks as he watched her, his voice throbbing with an emotion she didn't want to name. "I've waited ten years, and in those years you have refused to take my desire for you, or my needs, seriously, let alone your own. Tonight, you will take those needs seriously. You'll take me seriously, Ella."

Had she ever seen him look so powerful, so commanding? Suddenly, she felt much younger than him, and definitely much less experienced. His command of his own power, his own control, went beyond age or experience, and entered that unknown realm of supreme self-confidence. He knew what he was doing, she realized suddenly. James had a plan, just as he always had, she knew now. But why and what that the plan was, she couldn't decide.

"No other men." She shook her head, her hand trembling as she pushed her fingers through her hair. "I mean it, James. No one else."

His lips quirked. "You no longer set your own limits, Ella. I do. You'll learn that tonight. Whatever I want, however I want it, and you'll love it. Or you can continue to be a coward and deny what I know you feel for me. If that's the case, my bags are packed. Set them on the porch and I'll never bother you again."

She stared up at him, fear suddenly shaking her soul. "So I'm part of an orgy or I'm nothing to you, period?" she asked him, feeling her heart thunder in her chest. But what really terrified her was the clench of arousal that rippled through her cunt.

"No, Ella. I would never put you in the middle of an orgy," he promised her smoothly. "What I will put you in the middle of is more pleasure than you've known could exist. Pleasure I know you want. Need. Even now, after the past three days, you aren't satisfied. You climax until you nearly pass out with the pleasure of it, but you need more. And, by God, tonight I'll make sure you have what you need, or I won't bother trying anymore. I love you, Ella. Love you until my heart breaks with it, but I won't beg you, and I won't let you deny either of our needs. Now think about that."

Shock exploded through her body as he turned and left the room. She could feel her face paling, her body weakening at a knowledge he had possessed, and yet she hadn't.

It made sense now. James wasn't a man to chase after any woman, to care one way or the other if his desires weren't returned. Yet, he had chased her for ten years. Not in an obvious, lovesick manner, but in his own controlled, brooding way. He had made her aware of her own body, her own desires, even as she tried to hide from them, and made her more than aware of him.

She bit her lip, staring at the door, remembering his driving demands, his loss of control the night before. No other woman had managed that. Had it happened, she would have known about it. And his need for her wasn't diminishing. Like hers, it seemed to be growing stronger.

Even after the excesses of the past days, the fiery heat and lust that flared between them. He was right, she had kept reaching for more. Something, some unknown dark desire kept pushing her.

She shook her head, fighting the awakening realization. For years she had fought Jase, not because she secretly wanted what he offered, but because he didn't satisfy her. He didn't bring her to the mindless orgasms James could. He didn't make her pussy drench with a look. His needs hadn't filled her with this strange excitement and nervousness. She had never wanted to break the control he thought he had.

She eased from the bed and walked slowly to the shower. A cool shower. She needed to think, she needed to make sense of the past and of the present. But more than anything, she had to decide if the desires that filled James were truly a part of her own needs, or just a part of her desperation to keep him now that she had held him. She had to know, before she took the chance of losing him forever.

Chapter Twelve

ꟹ

"I need to talk to you." Of the five friends Ella had kept over the years, Terrie was perhaps the freest; the one Ella felt would be the most likely to understand her present predicament.

Silence met her request for long minutes. "Charlie called this morning, too," Terrie finally said softly. "Are you okay?"

Ella closed her eyes. Of course Charlie had called. Terrie, and Marey and most likely Pamela as well. Just what she needed, everyone to know who and what she was doing. Her parents would know, too, if they were still alive. Poor Charlie, she couldn't keep anything from their small group of friends, no matter how hard she tried.

"I'm fine," she finally whispered. "I just need to talk."

"I'll be right over then." She could almost hear Terrie's sharp nod.

Ella hung up the phone, sighing deeply. Terrie would know James the best. She had been married to one of his two brothers, the bastard. Ella, for one, was glad to see his final demise. Thomas Wyman had been a stone cold prick.

As she waited for the other woman to arrive, Ella made sweet iced tea, moved about the kitchen preparing glasses and fought to ignore the heat in her rear. The plug was driving her crazy. Her panties were damned near drenched from the moist heat of her pussy and no matter what she did her nipples wouldn't soften and just go the hell away. The scrape of the light cotton fabric of her sundress over them was about to drive her to distraction.

It wasn't long before she heard the front door open then close, and Terrie's voice calling out her name from the hall.

"I'm in the kitchen." For as long as Ella could remember, the kitchen was the favored spot for her and her friends to talk, to argue, to visit. Either over coffee or sweet tea, it was there they seemed to find the most comfort.

She set the glasses of ice and the pitcher of tea on the table as Terrie swept into the room. She stopped inside the doorway, looking around curiously. "Is the boy toy in residence today?"

Ella winced at the question, though it could have been the tight, erotic tugging of the plug in her rear as she sat down, she thought.

"James went somewhere," she sighed. "He didn't say where."

"He's meeting Jesse for lunch." Terrie shrugged as she sat down across from her. "Jesse was supposed to come over to the house and fix the faucet for me but James had some kind of emergency."

Ella watched her friend suspiciously. "Are you sleeping with him?"

"James?" Terrie's eyes widened in surprise.

"No, not James," she bit out. "Jesse. I know you're not sleeping with James, you would have killed him by now."

Terrie poured the glasses of tea and slid one closer to Ella. "Jesse isn't like James, Ella."

Ella lifted her brows at that surprising statement. "Have you lost your mind, Terrie?" she asked her carefully. "I caught him with Cole and Tessa. You are aware of this, right?"

"Well, Ella, you were so drunk that night when you called us over that you couldn't keep it to yourself," Terrie sighed regretfully. "I am aware that he likes to play. But he's not all dominant and fierce like Cole and James are. Jesse's softer."

Ella snorted. Terrie hadn't seen Jesse, her beloved brother-in-law, that day as he lay beneath Tess, obviously spurting his release inside her. The man was just as dominant as his brother. He just hid it from Terrie. The reasons he would do so worried Ella. Terrie didn't need more heartbreak, or more pain.

"I'm not here to talk about Jesse anyway," Terrie reminded her. "We're here to talk about you and James."

Ella was smart enough to recognize the same denial tactics she had used herself with James. She sighed wearily. Maybe Terrie was the wrong friend to call.

* * * * *

Maybe Jesse was the wrong brother to call. Unfortunately, James thought, he was his only brother. Even when Thomas had been alive, Jesse was still the only brother he had to talk to. The only other person he trusted.

"I love her, Jesse. What if she won't accept it?" James couldn't get the thought out of his mind.

His sexuality was a part of him, a part he didn't want to change, and saw no reason to change. Could he have been so wrong about Ella? Was he mistaking the excitement, the unspoken challenge she tempted him with? Could he do without watching another man fuck her? He could, it wasn't about sharing her. Besides, it wouldn't be a common thing. He wasn't that depraved. He wanted his woman to himself. And only one man. He had already discussed it with the one he had chosen to introduce her into the pleasures of a threesome. But could she accept it?

James was well aware that Charlie had, in depth, given Ella all the gossip she thought she had on the Trojans. He snorted silently. The ninny who had pinned that name on them didn't have the sense God gave a goose. Unfortunately, one of the leading members of the unofficial group had married her. He sighed wearily.

Whatever name you put to it, they were a group, of sorts. Nearly a dozen men who had met in college, and over the course of several years had gravitated together based on their sexual practices and their need to discuss and learn from each other's mistakes. There had been many. Often due to a member's unlucky choice of a lover who refused or even reviled their dominance. At present, there were eight of them, all in their thirties, all still looking for that one woman who could accept them.

Jesse leaned back in his chair, tipping his beer back and taking a healthy drink as James watched him. Finally, he shrugged. "She most likely knows what's coming, James. Ella can be a pure witch when she's riled. If she hasn't cut your balls off yet, then most likely she's not going to."

James winced. That didn't do much to reassure him. He tipped his own beer back, staring up at the ceiling of Jesse's home as he contemplated the coming evening. He had called Saxen earlier to set the time to meet him at Ella's home, and as that time rapidly approached, he found he was becoming more nervous than he had thought he would be.

"Saxen was my choice for tonight," he informed his brother quietly.

Jesse nodded slowly. "He's a good choice."

The tall, dark-skinned engineer worked with them at Delacourte Electronics as well, and was one of the most dependable men James knew.

He had spent over an hour talking to Jesse and getting nowhere. He wasn't any closer to stilling the nerves running riot inside him than he was to begin with.

"You have been of absolutely no help whatsoever," he finally sighed as he set the empty bottle on the glass coffee table and rose to his feet to leave. "Remind me of this when you finally decide to get off your ass and make your move on Terrie."

Jesse grunted as he rose to his feet to his feet. "Damned women. What did we do to deserve them?"

James shook his head. "I would say we were just lucky, but I'm starting to wonder about that one."

Chapter Thirteen

ꕤ

His bags weren't sitting on the porch. James pulled in behind Saxen's Mustang and breathed out a hard sigh of relief. He'd be damned, but he had never been this nervous in his life. His entire future, his relationship with Ella and his own needs were riding on this final day. If she turned him away, would he have the strength to stay in control and to walk away from one of the most important aspects of his sexuality?

He would if he had to. He admitted that to himself. Ella was more important than his desire, more important than his life. But he knew if he allowed it to happen, then neither of them would ever know complete fulfillment. That was his main concern. He knew Ella, better sometimes than she knew herself, and he knew she needed the extreme boundaries of sex just as intensely as he needed it for her. Pulling the keys from the ignition, he opened the door and stepped out of the car as Sax unfolded his tall frame from the other car.

"You need a bigger car, Sax." James repeated the comment he made every time he watched the other man slide from the low-slung car.

"James, that's my baby," Sax grinned, his teeth flashing white against his dark skin as he ran his hand over his slick, shaved head.

The sleek, little blue car was indeed one of his prized possessions, though he could have afforded better. That and the Harley. Sax had a set number of priorities. He had achieved all but one. Poor man, Sax had his eye set on a woman that wasn't about to let him anywhere near her. She would make his life hell, James knew.

"She might throw us out of the house." James paused at the bottom of the steps as he glanced at Sax. "She might shoot us."

Sax chuckled. "If you're brave enough to go after this one, James, then she should be brave enough to accept you. You've gotten this far without frostbite. I bet you last through the night."

Ella's nickname, The Ice Queen, had followed her even after her divorce to Jase.

"Frostbite?" James murmured as he shook his head. "That's the least of our worries, Sax."

He opened the door and stepped inside. He had left explicit instructions for her in the letter he had left in the living room before he went to Jesse's. He had been careful not to voice those instructions for fear of her outright rejection. If she didn't want this, then the luggage on the porch would have been a more humane way to cut his heart from his chest. Of course, a bullet would be more permanent.

"She should be in her room," he murmured. "Either restrained to the bed or waiting with the gun."

Sax chuckled behind him, and in the sound James could feel the other man's excitement. Sax was one of the few men who hadn't known Ella during her marriage to Jase. He had wanted his partner in this next experience with Ella to be free of any preconceived notions or ideas of loyalty. Ella was his. Sax would continue to join in periodic threesomes with him and Ella if this first session went as James hoped.

Just as Jesse would continue with Cole and Tess until he took that final step in securing his own woman. After marriage, there was no need, no desire to touch another woman. The commitment was strong, the need so extreme that other women held no attraction. It was often a confusing, hotly debated issue among the men who shared in this lifestyle. The need to see their women experiencing that pleasure of an added element to their sexuality. The periodic addition of another man, and in one case he knew of, another woman.

He stopped at Ella's bedroom door, took a deep breath and opened it slowly as Sax leaned against the doorframe. God help him. He nearly came in his slacks. She had buckled the straps to her ankles as he ordered, and her arm into one of the wrist restraints. She was staring at the ceiling, her breathing hard and rough as he walked slowly into the room.

He moved to the free wrist restraint and bent over to buckle it slowly. He caressed her wrist, feeling the hard throb of blood in the vein beneath her skin. She gazed up at him, a shade of fear mixing with the excitement in her gaze.

"Are you sure, Ella?" He sat on the side of the bed, cupping her cheek gently as he stared down at her.

She was trembling. He could feel the fear and excitement traveling through her. It would heighten the sensations, he knew; make the arousal, the coming orgasm more intense, hotter and brighter. He could barely hold back his own anticipation. He had waited, longed for this more years than he could count.

"No." She breathed out roughly. "I'm not sure of anything right now, James. Don't ask me questions like that."

His lips quirked into a soft, gentle smile. Despite her words, he could see that she was more than ready. Her breasts were swollen, her nipples hard little points atop the firm mounds.

"You'll only be restrained until we think you're ready to be released," he promised her softly as he stood by the bed and began to undress.

The word "we" had a small, strangled whimper escaping her throat. He watched the shiver that worked over her body, the way her nipples tightened, hardened further.

"Is the plug still inside you?" he asked her gently as he dropped his shirt to the floor, aware that Sax was slowly undressing behind him.

"No." Her voice was low, breathless. "You told me to take it out."

"You followed my directions exactly?" He kept his voice firm, stern.

Her eyes were wide, dark as she watched him, careful not to look toward his hips. Nervousness and excitement had her body quivering on a finely balanced edge of desire and lust.

"Exactly." Her voice trembled.

He stripped off his pants and boxers, his hand going to the near-to-bursting erection that stood out from his body. He was so damned hard he knew he wouldn't make it five minutes if he didn't find relief soon. A relief he knew her sweet, suckling mouth would provide him.

"Sax, loosen the chains on the footboard. I need her sweet mouth first, or I won't make it."

"I don't blame you. She's beautiful, James." Sax spoke for the first time as he moved to the bed, his own cock thick and hard as he stared down at Ella.

Her gaze flickered to him, her eyes widening as they caught the sight of his cock, as hard and long as James, if not a bit more. Her gaze flew up to him and he could see the fear in her eyes.

"I'm scared," she whispered, her hands curling into fists as he sat down beside her on the bed again.

"The fear is good, to a point, Ella," he told her gently. "You have to trust me, though. You have to trust that I won't allow you to be harmed, that I will never threaten you, never cause you undue pain in any way. Without that trust, baby, we're wasting our time here."

His hand reached out to cup one of her full breasts, his fingers gripping the nipple firmly. She breathed in roughly, the little point tightening further. Leaning to her, he drew one of the hard points into his mouth, relishing the thick moan that vibrated at her throat.

When his head rose, he was pleased to see the flush of lust, of deepening desire coloring her once pale face.

"I love you, Ella," he said softly. "Above all things, I love you."

She nodded her head sharply. "Fine. Fine." She was breathing hard and deep, then her eyes widened, shock flaring in her expression as her gaze went between her thighs.

James followed her look and his lips quirked into a smile. Sax couldn't resist soft, wet pussy, and he was lapping at the creamy mound now with the intent concentration of a man enjoying a prized dessert.

He couldn't help but watch, and Sax gave a show worthy of any porn star as he made certain each touch, each stroke could be clearly seen. His tongue ran through the narrow slit, parting it, gathering the thick juices on the tip of it before he licked them into his mouth and started again. Slow, teasing strokes of his tongue that circled her pink pearl clit then returned to her tender opening to start all over again.

Then his fingers parted her, his dark flesh an erotic contrast to her pale skin. When he had her lips flared open, his tongue distended then disappeared slowly inside her vagina. James's cock jerked at the sight of it, imagining the feel of her pussy gripping the other man's tongue, her muscles rippling around it as he fucked in and out of the hot channel.

"James." He saw her hips jerk, the muscles of her abdomen tightening as her body tensed, her legs moving against the restraints.

Sax was slurping on her now, sucking as much of the thick honey from between her thighs that he could reach. And James knew even more would replace it. It would be impossible to suck that well of sweetness dry.

"Shhh." James leaned forward, his tongue licking over her lips as she stared up at him with dark, shocked eyes. "Just enjoy, Ella. Just enjoy."

He kissed her. A long, wet kiss that had her moaning into his lips, her head lifting from the pillow as she fought to get closer. Sax's noisy feast below seemed to make the kiss more desperate, heated, as her body began to clamor for release. A release she would be screaming for before it ever came.

His lips moved from hers, his own breathing rough, impatient, as they traveled down her neck, moving unerringly to the hard-tipped breasts that rose and fell roughly. She was moaning, her head thrashing on the pillow as she fought to get closer to the mouths tormenting her.

Sax would tease her. He wouldn't want her release coming until she was sandwiched between them, no more than James did. And she would be ready for them. Then he heard her shocked gasp, the moan of near pain that erupted from her throat and knew Sax was preparing her back entrance as he stroked her cunt hotter.

"It's okay, baby." He kissed her nipple, licking it gently as he rose to his knees beside her. "Just enjoy, Ella. Just let it feel good."

He gripped his cock in his hand, grimacing at the near black of her eyes, the flush of lust on her face. She was so beautiful it was damned near killing him.

"James, I can't stand it." She bucked against Sax's mouth as James looked to the other man.

Sax had pulled back, watching as two of his fingers sank slowly in her pussy, two up the forbidden depths of her anus. Her heels were pressed into the mattress, fighting for leverage to thrust against the shallow thrusts. Sax wasn't about to hurry, though. He knew as well as James did, the pleasure she would experience from the teasing.

Sax's head lowered again then, unable to keep his lips, his tongue from the soaked slit that flowered open for him. He murmured his enjoyment into her flesh, his eyes closing as he savored each lick. James felt his cock drip with his own pre-cum at the sight. Her moans, her ragged breaths, the unconscious sexuality reflecting in her face, in her jerky movements, was more than he could bear. If he didn't push his swollen cock into her mouth soon he was going to go insane.

Chapter Fourteen

ജ

Ella wanted to scream, to find some way to release the surging sensations building in her body, but she couldn't find the breath. Seconds later the choice was taken out of her hands as James's cock slipped past her lips, filling her mouth, as his rough groan echoed around her.

Her lips tightened on him, her tongue licking over the thick veins, the tight flesh in greedy hunger, as the scents and sounds of sexual need wrapped around her. The flared head of his erection sank nearly to her throat as her tongue worked desperately along the shaft. She suckled him, pulling her head back then pushing forward, tempting him to fuck her mouth, to spill the hot rich seed that tasted like nectar on her tongue.

Between her thighs, Sax was lapping at her cunt, his tongue dipping into her vagina, two large fingers sliding deep inside her anus. She shuddered with the sensation, moaning around the flesh thrusting between her lips as she fought to suckle it, to tempt him into the release she knew he was teetering on the edge of.

She was suspended on a rack of agonizing pleasure and desperate fear. She had seen the other man's cock, thick and hard, the dark flesh appearing angry, eager to take her. How would she bear it? How would her body hold two thick shafts like that at the same time?

"Ella, you're killing me." James's voice was thick and deep as his hand gripped the halfway point of his cock and his thrusts became harder. "Your mouth is so sweet, so hot."

She felt the head pulse against her tongue as she delved beneath it to the sensitive spot that she knew would make him groan with dark lust. The sound shot to her womb, ripping through her with almost climactic intensity. She tightened her mouth on him, slurping on his hard flesh hungrily as his thrusts became harder, his breathing rougher.

He was on the edge of release, she could feel it, almost taste it, but she was as well, and the tormentor between her thighs was refusing to send her over. She strained against his suckling mouth, his piercing tongue, but nothing seemed to be enough.

She growled around James' cock as she fought for that one stroke, that one caress, that would send her over the edge.

"Stay still." A sudden, light slap to her mound as the other man moved back had her stilling in surprise.

Her eyes flew to James's face as he watched her, then glanced down once again.

"Again." James voice was soft. "She's not sucking me properly, Sax. I think she needs to be punished for it."

Her mouth was full of James's cock, but her strangled scream should have been enough. When the lightly stinging blow landed, she felt her entire body flinch. Not from pain, but from shameful pleasure. Her clit throbbed, pulsed, so swollen and sensitive now that the light blow was agony and ecstasy all in one.

Her mouth tightened on James's cock, her tongue stroking, her mouth suckling as she knew he liked it, but she was determined that when the restraints came off, so did her façade of submission. This was all well and good, but she would make certain they both paid for the tormenting arousal.

Another blow landed. She jerked, moaning in protest at the streaking sensations. Her clit swelled further, throbbing in an agony of arousal. When the next blow came, she growled around the cock thrusting into her mouth and raised her hips for more. More. One more blow aimed just right, and her clit would explode.

But the next smack never came. Instead his tongue stroked, caressed, running around her clit with light, deliberately teasing strokes. She rewarded James, the beast, with a firmer suction on his erection, driving him past his own control.

"Yes, Ella. Baby. I'm going to come now. Take me, Ella." He powered in, his moan deep and hard as his cock suddenly exploded.

Thick and hot, his seed shot into her mouth as his body jerked with the pleasure she knew was washing over him. In return, the mouth on her cunt only teased her more. She continued to suckle James's flesh, drawing the last drop of his tangy seed from the tip as she fought to keep from screaming out in agony.

"Perfect." James pulled back from her, his cock still hard, leaving her suckling mouth reluctantly.

Perspiration coated his body. His eyes were dark, his face flushed, his lips heavy with sensuality as his hands went to her breasts once again.

"Are you ready, baby?" His hands went to the restraints at her wrists as Sax moved away from her to loosen those at her ankles.

Ella shuddered. Her pussy was on fire, desperate, yearning. Every nerve ending in her body was sensitized and throbbing for release. When they released her, Sax moved to the side of the bed, laying back, the bulging length of his heavily veined cock rising to his abdomen. As she watched, he rolled a condom over the throbbing shaft, preparing to take her.

Ella moved, coming quickly to her knees as she caught James's shoulders, her hands moving to his head as she pressed her lips to his. The surprising action seemed to fray his hard-won control. His tongue plunged into her mouth as she felt him moving her, Sax lifting her.

They lifted her over Sax's big body until she felt the wide, flared head of his cock nudging at her vagina. She pulled back then, staring up at James, seeing the heady excitement in his gaze as the other man clasped her hips, holding her still.

"I'll take you anally first," he whispered. "Then Sax will take you. Scream for me, Ella. Don't worry about control, don't worry about anything. Just the pleasure."

She groaned as Sax drew her down to him, his lips whispering over her cheek, her neck, as he drew her head to his hard shoulder. Below, his cock throbbed at the opening of her cunt

"Relax, Ella," Sax's voice was soft, soothing. "It's like nothing else you'll ever experience. Nothing else you'll ever know."

She flinched as she felt two fingers, slick and cool, slide into the prepared depths of her anus. She cried out, pressing closer, desperate to drive the hard cock inside her pussy as James tormented her back entrance.

"Stay still, Ella." Sax's fingers tightened at her hips. "Patience, beautiful. Patience."

Then James moved into position. She felt the head of his cock nudge against the little puckered hole a second before he began to press inside. She tried to arch, but Sax held her close and still. Her wail, one of agonizing arousal and the sharp bite of erotic pain, was muffled against the shoulder beneath her as James entered her with excruciating slowness.

"James," she cried out his name as Sax's hands held her still, closer, his cock throbbing at the portal of her cunt.

She felt the burning stretch of tight muscles, heard James groan, praising the heat and the grip of her tight channel. One hand gripped a buttock, flexing, tightening on her as he surged inside her last few inches with a hard, shockingly deep groan.

Impaled, stretched and overfilled, Ella fought to breathe through the first fiery thrust, then to adjust to the invasion. She tightened on his cock, her breaths beseeching cries as her cunt flooded with moisture, convulsed and fought for release.

"Now," James groaned behind her. "Now, Sax, I won't last long."

"Please." She felt the condom-covered tip of his cock force its way into the entrance of her pussy.

She bucked against them, the heat and hardness searing her, the pleasure/pain more than she could bear as he worked his cock inside her by slow degrees.

She tried to thrash in their arms, tried to force Sax to enter her faster, harder, dying for the orgasm she knew was just out of reach.

"James. Damn. She's tight." He groaned beneath her as he rocked inside her, the slick inner juice easing his way, but not by much.

As each agonizing inch pressed into her cunt, she could feel James, thicker, harder, as he throbbed inside her ass.

"Almost there," Sax groaned. "Hold on, baby, I'm giving it all to you."

She screamed, loud and deep, as the last inches powered inside her with a strong surge of his hips, burying his erection into her to the hilt. A second later, James began to move behind her.

The sounds of wet sex, desperate cries and hard male groans filled the air as Ella shuddered, her body jerking almost spasmodically in the grip of a lust she could have never imagined. The two men, their thrusts perfectly timed, began to fuck her with hard, driving strokes. Muscles protested, flared with heat, but parted beneath the driving strokes of the two thick shafts possessing her.

Between them, Ella cried out their names repeatedly, pushing herself into each thrust, flying higher, surging deeper into the ecstatic orgasm she knew was building faster, harder inside her.

Their thrusts quickened then, pushing into her body with rapid movements, rasping her clit against the wiry roughness of Sax's pubic hair until the moment insanity hit. She felt her mind, her heart, her womb and her pussy explode. Convulsively, simultaneously, as her scream rocked the air between them. Behind her, James stiffened at that moment, his hot seed flooding her anus as Sax thrust into her tightening pussy one last time and tightened, his groan of release sounding hard and loud at her ear.

"Ella, baby." James leaned over her, holding her close as she continued to cry out, her body shuddering so harshly she feared she would break apart.

"James," she cried out his name, tears wetting her face as another vibration wracked her body, tightening her, blinding her. She tightened on the cocks still filling her, riding her through the mindless orgasm until she collapsed, boneless, against Sax's body.

"Ella. God. Baby." James pulled her from Sax, easing her into his arms as he fell to the bed, holding her close, tight, as the other man moved from the bed.

Ella could still feel the internal shudders racing through her womb, her own release dripping from her cunt as James rocked her, his lips caressing her face, his hands stroking her back.

"Don't leave me." She burrowed closer against his chest, too exhausted to hold him to her, praying he would hold her to him instead.

"Never," he whispered at her ear, his vow echoing to her soul. "Never, Ella. I'll always be here."

Chapter Fifteen

ഇ

"She asleep?" Sax was waiting in the kitchen, dressed, looking smartly presentable. He didn't look as though he'd spent the last hours helping James fuck Ella into another screaming climax. James had held her in his arms, stroking her body, easing her through the destructive shudders of her orgasm before moving to take her again himself.

After the first violent sensations had eased from her body, neither man had been able to leave her in peace. She responded to each touch, each stroke of their hands as though it were the first time.

"She's asleep." James nodded, wishing he were as well. He had never been so exhausted in his life.

"Will she be okay?" Sax glanced back at the hallway that led to her bedroom, a frown shaping his brow.

"She'll be fine." James was sure of that. Her sleepily muttered words as she finally gave into her own exhaustion assured him of it.

"Well, you waited long enough for her." Sax rolled his broad shoulders as he headed for the hallway. "I'm heading home now. I need to sleep."

James followed him to the door and as the other man turned back to him, lifted a brow questioningly.

"I'll need your help now," Sax said with a fierce frown. "You and Cole set up Ella's downfall. I expect your help setting up my woman's fall."

James grinned. "You have a deal, Sax. Give me a chance to figure out how to get to her, and I'll let you know."

Sax nodded. "I'll be waiting. Impatiently, but waiting."

He walked out the front door, closing it softly behind him. James sighed deeply, secured the locks and then returned to Ella's bedroom.

She was in the same position he had left her in, curled up on her side, her auburn hair a cloud of silk around her face, her expression peaceful, serene. Had he ever seen her peaceful or serene before he invaded her life? He shook his head, knowing he hadn't.

"Is he gone?" she mumbled as he eased into the bed beside her.

Surprised, James stared down at her closed eyes.

"He's gone." He pulled her into his arms, tucking the blankets around her again.

Her voice was drowsy, replete, as she snuggled against him. "No more threesomes." She yawned. "I can't move."

He chuckled gently. "Let me know when you need to move and I'll do it for you," he assured her.

Silence thickened around them again for long seconds.

"What now?" she asked, her voice even, though he heard the worry in her tone.

"Hmm. Many things." He smiled against her hair. "But I'm not leaving, Ella. Not now, not ever. You're mine. You submitted to it, baby. You can't back out now."

The letter he had left that day was detailed in more than one regard. Submit now, submit for life. The ring that had accompanied it graced her finger, just where it belonged.

"You have a lousy way of proposing, James. I'm going to have to teach you better. Boy toys are supposed to be more romantic, especially married ones." Warmth filled her voice, a warmth that gave him hope. Then joy swelled in his chest when she whispered, "Especially the one I love."

He laughed then, feeling freer, happier than he could ever remember feeling.

"I'll keep that in mind, baby." He kissed her lips tenderly, feeling her smile, her exhausted response. "Sleep now. In my arms, Ella. The way it's supposed to be."

And they both slept.

Epilogue

ꟗ

He had sworn she would come to him. He wouldn't spend agonizing months trying to ease her into a relationship she had stated she would never tolerate. So he tried to seduce her into it instead.

After Thomas's death, he had made himself indispensable to her. He was at the house often, fixing this or that, just talking or watching movies late into the night. Despite appearances, Terrie was a wary person, well aware of how easily she could be hurt, how weak she was physically. From what he had gathered, his brother had been more of a bastard than he had ever imagined.

"Now that was a beautiful wedding." Terrie stumbled against him a bit as he helped her into the house.

James and Ella's wedding ceremony had made her teary-eyed, reflective. She had sat in the limo on the way home, quiet, a bit sad, staring out the window as her fingers stroked over the upper swell of one breast that her cream-colored dress had revealed. The action had caused his cock to swell, to harden in agonized need.

"Well, it wasn't a long one, anyway." Jesse pulled her to him, leading her to the living room, enjoying her soft weight against his side.

The soft silk of her dress slid against his hands, and when he sat her on the couch, the hem rode just below the crotch of her panties. Cream-colored as well, silk. He was betting it was a thong.

"You kissed the bride." Her surprising comment had his brows lifting in surprise.

He had kissed the bride. Long and deep, to her complete surprise and shocked arousal.

"Yeah, I did." He knelt at her feet, removing the high-heeled shoes from her small feet.

"That was so decadent," she bit out. "Kissing her that way, with your tongue. You made her horny."

He smothered his laughter. "That was the point," he whispered up at her as he caressed the slight welts on the side of her foot.

She pouted. She had such an intriguing pout, and used it on him often.

"I promise not to kiss Ella again." His hand stroked her calf as he felt a small tremor work over her body.

"Sax fucked her. He was at the wedding, of course," she bit out. "I knew she couldn't hold out. She gave in too easily."

She sounded angry with Ella, though Jesse knew she was more than happy that her friend had finally found some happiness.

"You, of course, would be much harder to convince?" he asked her, careful to keep his voice even, his hand on her calf comforting rather than arousing.

She leveled a hard look at him. "I am not so easy."

That was sure as hell the truth. He murmured consoling words, though, massaging her foot, well aware of how the heels made her feet ache.

"I'm not your sister." She jerked her foot from his grasp, staring down at him angrily. "Stop treating me like one."

"Keep it up and I'll turn you over my knee and paddle your ass." He jerked her foot back. "Now what has you so upset? I thought you were happy for Ella."

"I am." She was pouting again, watching him darkly.

"Then what's your problem?" he asked her again.

"You've never kissed me like that," she finally bit out, her cheeks blooming with a flush. "Why haven't you?"

He pursed his lips. Her breasts were moving quickly beneath her dress, her nipples hard, poking impatiently at the light fabric. He allowed his hand to stroke higher along the inside of her leg.

"Because," he whispered, "I can never decide where to put my tongue first."

She blinked, confusion filling her expression. "What?" Her question was almost a gasp.

"You heard me." His hand stroked to her thigh. "Do I take your lips and plunge my tongue into your mouth, Terrie, or do I push it as deep and as hard up your pussy as I can, and suck all that sweet cream into my mouth? Deciding is a bitch."

Her mouth opened, her thighs tensed. He watched as she fought to breathe, to draw in air to counter the arousal he saw surging in her gaze. He parted her thighs then, his cock jerking at the sight of the damp spot on the silk of her panties. His gaze rose back to hers.

"Do you want that, Terrie? My mouth buried in your cunt, my tongue fucking you to orgasm?" Her thighs opened farther as a strangled moan whispered past her throat.

"Please," she whispered, and his cock surged in joy then throbbed in disappointment as he gently closed her thighs.

"Remind me when you're sober, Terrie." He stood to his feet, staring down at her shocked expression. "I won't fuck you drunk. Sober up, then call me. But don't be surprised if you find out exactly why Sax was at that wedding, and what he's most likely doing right now to your friend's climaxing body. You won't play with me, Terrie," he warned her softly.

He turned and left the room, then the house. If he didn't, he knew he would fuck her, knew he would drive his cock so deep and hard inside her she would scream for her orgasm. And he couldn't. Not yet. She hadn't seduced him; she didn't want it enough. When she did, well then, he grinned, then he would give her everything he had ever dreamed she could take.

SEDUCTION

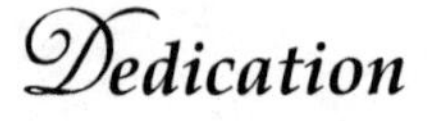

Dedication

ꕥ

For a wonderful writer and friend,

Marly Chance.

Thank you so much for the support and the encouragement you've given, and for your kind words. You have inspired me as a writer and as a friend. Thank you for everything.

Prologue

ℬ

Jesse had sworn Terrie would come to him. He wouldn't spend agonizing months trying to ease her into a relationship she had stated she would never tolerate. So he tried to seduce her into it instead.

After Jesse's brother, Thomas, died he had made himself indispensable to her. He was at the house often, fixing this or that, just talking or watching movies late into the night. Despite appearances, Terrie was a wary person, well aware of how easily she could be hurt, how weak she was physically. From what he had gathered, his brother had been more of a bastard than he had ever imagined.

Thomas had hurt her in the worst possible way. Terrie could have overcome physical abuse. She would have just left. But the systematic psychological and verbal abuse had damned near destroyed her.

"Now that was a beautiful wedding." Terrie stumbled against him a bit as he helped her into the house.

James and Ella's wedding ceremony had made her teary-eyed, reflective. She had sat in the limo on the way home, quiet, a bit sad, staring out the window as her fingers stroked over the upper swell of one breast her cream-colored dress had revealed. The action had caused his cock to swell—to harden in agonizing need.

Jesse's brother, James, had married her best friend after nearly tens years of waiting impatiently on Ella to come around and be tempted by the sexuality he offered her.

"Well, it wasn't a long one, anyway." Jesse pulled her to him, leading her to the living room, enjoying her soft weight against his side.

The smooth silk of her dress slid against his hands, and when he sat her on the couch, the hem rode just below the crotch of her panties. Cream-colored silk as well. He was betting it was a thong.

"You kissed the bride." Her surprising comment had his brows lifting in surprise.

He had kissed the bride. Long and deep, to her complete surprise and shocked arousal.

"Yeah, I did." He knelt before her, removing the high-heeled shoes from her small feet.

"That was so decadent," she sighed then. "Kissing her that way, with your tongue. You made her horny."

He smothered his laughter. "That was the point," he whispered up at her as he caressed the slight welts on the side of her foot.

She pouted. She had such an intriguing pout, and used it on him often.

"I promise not to kiss Ella again." His hand stroked her calf as he felt a small tremor work over her body.

"Sax fucked her. He was at the wedding, of course." She shot him a narrow eyed, disgruntled look. "I knew she couldn't hold out. She gave in too easily."

She sounded angry with Ella, though Jesse knew she was more than pleased that her friend had finally found some happiness.

"You, of course, would be much harder to convince?" he asked her, careful to keep his voice even, his hand on her calf comforting rather than arousing.

She leveled a hard look at him. "I am not so easy."

That was sure as hell the truth. He murmured consoling words while massaging her foot, well aware of how the heels made her feet ache.

"I'm not your sister." She jerked her foot from his grasp, staring down at him angrily. "Stop treating me like one."

"Keep it up and I'll turn you over my knee and paddle your ass." He jerked her foot back. "Now what has you so upset? I thought you were happy for Ella."

"I am." She was pouting again, watching him darkly.

"Then what's your problem?" he asked her again.

"You've never kissed me like that," she finally said, her cheeks blooming with a flush. "Why haven't you?"

Her hazel eyes, more green than brown, watched him with narrow frustration and arousal. Her soft red hair cascaded around her face, the fiery waves tempting his hands to smooth them back from her flushed cheeks.

He pursed his lips. Her breasts were moving quickly beneath her dress, her nipples hard, poking impatiently at the light fabric. He allowed his hand to stroke higher along the inside of her leg.

"Because," he whispered, "I can never decide where to put my tongue first."

She blinked, confusion filling her expression. "What?" Her question was almost a gasp.

"You heard me." His hand stroked to her thigh. "Do I take your lips and plunge my tongue into your mouth, Terrie, or do I push it as deep and as hard up your pussy as I can, and suck all that sweet cream into my mouth? Deciding is a bitch."

Her mouth opened, her thighs tensed. He watched as she fought to breathe, to draw in air to counter the arousal he saw surging in her gaze. He parted her thighs then, his cock jerking at the sight of the damp spot on the silk of her panties. His gaze rose back to hers.

"Do you want that, Terrie? My mouth buried in your cunt, my tongue fucking you to orgasm?" Her thighs opened farther as a strangled moan whispered past her throat.

"Please," she whispered, and his cock surged in joy then throbbed in disappointment as he gently closed her thighs.

"Remind me when you're sober, Terrie." He stood to his feet, staring down at her shocked expression. "I won't fuck you drunk. Sober up, then call me. But don't be surprised if you find out exactly why Sax was at that wedding, and what he's most likely doing right now to your friend's climaxing body. You won't play with me, Terrie," he warned her softly.

He turned and left the room, then the house. If he didn't, he knew he would fuck her, knew he would drive his cock so deep and hard inside her she would scream for her orgasm. And he couldn't. Not yet. She hadn't seduced him; she didn't want it enough. When she did, well then—he grinned—then he would give her everything he had ever dreamed she could take.

Chapter One

ﻻ

Remind me when you're sober, Terrie. The words echoed through her head. *You won't play with me, Terrie.*

She pushed her fingers restlessly through her red hair as she paced the house. He had left hours before, and she was sober, but she couldn't find the nerve to pick up that damned phone. She was terrified.

You think I'm bad, her dead husband's sneering voice echoed around her. *I should give you a taste of Jesse, Terrie. Let him share you a time or two with his buddies. Maybe then you would appreciate me more.* She shuddered. She appreciated Thomas more dead.

She shook her head as she moved into the small kitchen. She was free of one Wyman and now looking at another. Was she insane? And what was worse, she was looking at Jesse. The same Jesse who had fucked her best friend's daughter. The same Jesse who had been her friend for the last three years. She shuddered as the thought repeated itself. She had to be crazy.

Jesse was part of a very select group of men. Tess, Ella's daughter was married to one of them: Cole, Jesse's best friend. Ella had walked into her ex-husband's home to find her daughter held between Jesse and Cole in the final throes of an intense ménage.

Terrie had known for years that Jesse was part of this group. There were eight of them. Intensely dominant, charismatic men whose lusts knew few bounds. One of their greater demands was the ménage. The complete surrender and submission of their lovers to the pleasures they could bring them.

Ella, it seemed, had finally given in as well. Tess's mother had been outraged, furious when she thought Jesse was actually his twin, James, fucking her daughter. She had nearly driven herself crazy with the pain. Loving one of those men was hell. Terrie knew this well.

Thankfully, James had grown tired of the wait and went after Ella in a way that left her little desire to fight him. Sax had been James's choice for the final sexual obstacle in his path with Ella.

Terrie sighed bleakly. First Tess and now Ella. The two people who meant the most to her had stepped into a relationship that inhabited only Terrie's darkest, most lust-filled dreams. The very thing that had driven her from accepting Jesse's attentions years before in favor of what she saw as the safer brother.

Terrie moved from the kitchen to the back deck, sitting in the chair swing as she stared out into the slowly darkening evening. Her body was on fire. She knew what Jesse was. Knew his desires and what he liked. She couldn't help but know. Thomas had been quite explicit in his description of them.

She curled her legs beneath her as the chair swayed softly with her weight. The soothing rhythm normally eased her stress, but tonight it seemed to only provoke it. The soft back and forth sway made her cunt clench with the thought of Jesse moving between her thighs, his cock thrusting into her hungry pussy with the same slow, steady movement.

She had sworn she would never allow herself to be shared, to be used by the man she loved. She remembered when Thomas first gleefully announced his brother's preferences as Jesse sat at their dinner table. Not that Terrie hadn't already been aware of them.

Terrie had been mortified by his drunken announcement, and more than shocked as Jesse sat back in his chair with that sardonic twist to his mouth and asked Thomas if he was trying to scare Terrie, or convince her to join in. It was then she learned that Thomas, too, had been part of the lifestyle Jesse enjoyed. Until he had married her.

She sighed wearily. Reliving the mistake her marriage had been wasn't going to help her. Jesse was her problem now, not Thomas. And Jesse and his brother were like night and day. Of course, she had known that when she married Thomas. It was her fault. She had married what she considered a safer alternative. And had learned better, nearly at the expense of her sanity.

But none of that solved her present problem. That problem being Jesse Wyman and his incredible stubbornness. Call him when she sobered up. She snorted. She hadn't been that drunk. She wasn't so stupid she didn't know Sax was joining Ella and James on their wedding night, either. Ella had confided that piece of news to her already.

God. Could she do it? Her pussy pulsed at the thought but all her previous beliefs screamed out in rejection of the idea. She knew Jesse would never go to another woman. Terrie had been with Ella when Tess imparted that information. The men wanted no one else. What they wanted was to see the women experience the pleasure of two men worshipping their bodies, glorying in their arousal.

Tess was more than happy with her marriage to Cole. Terrie's hands clenched in jealousy as she thought of the other woman. How many times had Jesse been in Tess's bed in the past year? How many times had he fucked her as Terrie lay aroused, dreaming of his touch. Touching herself because Jesse hadn't been there to touch her.

God, she was demented. She had lost any claim to sanity. Or had she?

She groaned at the futility of her own argument. It didn't matter, because fact was fact. There was no way in hell she could ask Jesse to fuck her with another man. There was no way she could seduce him…

So you're Jesse's lady. One of the men at the wedding had said as he had approached her. *I can see why he's dropped out of circulation now.*

Jesse had moved in then, steering her away from the grinning blonde who watched her with wicked green eyes. What had his name been? She frowned as she tried to remember. Lucian. Wasn't it Lucian? He didn't work at Delacourte's, she knew. Jesse had mentioned something about computers.

She snapped her fingers. Lucian Conover. He designed some kind of weird computer programs for the government, if she remembered correctly. Surely Jesse hadn't already approached someone? What did they do, sit around with their beers and discuss who would fuck their women?

Her face flushed. Good God, what the hell was she getting herself into? Couldn't he just fuck her? Would she settle for just being fucked?

"Dammit." She jumped from the chair and moved quickly to the phone just inside the house. Jerking it off the base she quickly punched in Jesse's number.

"Yes, Terrie." His voice was dark, smooth, like rich chocolate. She had an addiction for chocolate.

"Did you ask Lucian Conover to help you fuck me?" she asked him point blank. Beating around the bush had never been her strong suit.

Silence met her abrupt question. A long, drawn out silence that made her begin to wonder if he had hung the phone up on her.

"Jesse?" Her voice was sharp, but her knees weakened.

"No," he finally answered abruptly. "Not exactly. Are you sober now?"

There was a shade of worry in his tone now.

"Very much so," she snarled, thinking he was lucky she couldn't throw something at him. "How would you like it,

Jesse, if I approached one of my girlfriends to help me fuck you?"

Another silence. "Which one?" Was that curiosity in his voice? She almost rapped the phone against the table in irritation.

"You're a menace," she accused him heatedly. "And I've changed my mind. I don't want to fuck you at all, Jesse. Actually, Mr. Conover seemed rather interested." She checked her nails carefully as she considered the possibilities. "Maybe he's not into the sharing deal after all?"

Jesse cleared his throat. "Terrie, I wouldn't continue this way, if I were you."

"I bet he's hung, too," she said with apparent interest. "I hear he's quite good in bed. Maybe I'll find out. Good night, Jesse, and kiss my ass."

She disconnected abruptly. Damn him. She knew he had talked to Conover. He must have. She gritted her teeth furiously. Trojans. They were Trojans, all right. Trojan headaches.

The phone rang with a harsh, shrill note. Terrie jerked at the sound before picking it up and glanced at the caller display knowingly.

"Yes, Jesse?" she greeted him sweetly.

"I'll do more than kiss your ass, Terrie," he promised, his voice dark, arousing. "You should know better than to dare me, baby."

She felt a nervous shiver of anticipation work over her body. Her thighs clenched, the liquid heat of her vagina spilling from the lips of her cunt at the sound of his dark, deep voice. It rasped over the line, stroking her senses with erotic purpose.

"Get a life," she snorted. "I wasn't daring you, Jesse, I was merely making a statement of intent."

Silence sizzled over the line.

"You think you're so brave," he said, his voice gentle. So gentle, so filled with obvious affection, that she felt her throat tighten with emotion.

He could do that to her so easily. Have her furious, ready to flay him alive, then turn so soft, so incredibly tender she wanted to melt into a puddle of arousal at his feet.

"I am brave," she reminded him, determined she wouldn't be swayed this time.

She heard his disbelieving snort, as though he were trying to hide his disbelief.

"We'll see," he laughed gently. "Don't worry, baby. I won't press you on this. I want you, but I won't take something from you that you don't want to give. You're safe."

She frowned, biting her lips as she heard the regret in his voice. It was so like Jesse. The thought speared through her mind. Her heart. He was always so careful to be certain no one was hurt; that he gave rather than took from anyone. Would he pretend to want her to keep from hurting her? Or had he pretended he didn't want her to save her from something he felt she couldn't handle? With Jesse, it could have been either.

"You don't want me." She fought the bitterness that closed her throat. She was terrified that was her answer.

"Terrie, I'm dying to fuck you," he finally sighed. "I want you so damned bad my cock is hard enough to hammer nails. But I don't want you hurt. Not ever again, baby. And I'm afraid what I need would hurt you. Go to bed, baby. Don't worry about this. I promise, I still love you."

His abrupt about-face had tears stinging her eyes. He wanted her. She knew he did. But she would be damned if she would beg.

"You know, Jesse, there are times you aren't fit to kill," she snapped. "What makes you think I need your protection?"

"Terrie..."

"You go to bed, Jesse. See if you can sleep with that hard-on driving you crazy. And while you do, just remember. I offered. I won't do so again. And I still love you, too." And she realized in that moment just how much she did love Jesse.

She hung the phone up quickly. When it rang moments later, she watched it with narrow-eyed intent. She was a woman, not a child, and Jesse's insistence on treating her with kid gloves was getting on her nerves. It was time to show him...

She smiled slowly. Oh yes, it was definitely time to show him that he wasn't the only one who knew how to seduce. She could play the game just as well, and he was about to learn that lesson quite quickly.

Chapter Two

ꟓ

Terrie refused to let nerves or fear sway her. The time she had spent married to Thomas had curbed her natural responsiveness, her love of living, and she knew it. After the first month, he had refused to touch her. He had caustically broken down her confidence in herself and her sexuality. Nothing she did could please him. Each touch was dissected for faults and found wanting.

And he hadn't been gentle in his lack of desire for her. He had raged often, and with cruel emphasis on the fact that it was her fault. Hadn't he enjoyed sex before her, he would scream? She was destroying his manhood, destroying their lives with her inept responses. What man could want her? What man could desire her with the faults her body held? Her breasts were too large. Her legs were too short. Her hair was too thin. The list went on and on.

Of course, she had known, intellectually, that he was insane. Men had found her desirable before Thomas. But being unable to satisfy her husband, hearing daily his list of her shortcomings had damaged something inside her. If she couldn't please her husband, how could she ever hope to please anyone else?

The cycle had nearly destroyed her. Having him invite Jesse to the house often, throwing his sexual preferences in her face, then later, after his brother left, cruelly going into detail about how little she could please a man of Jesse's tastes, had almost broken her.

She had paid the ultimate price for her fear of Jesse's sexuality. It had been that fear that had driven her into the arms of his brother. A man she had believed was gentler, less inclined to dominate and demand her submission sexually. Sexually, Thomas had demanded the ultimate price. He hadn't wanted submission; he had wanted something far less gentle. Sexual slavery.

She shuddered as she smoothed the silk stockings up her legs and adjusted the elastic tops before standing to observe the effect in the full-length mirror. The black silk bra and thong contrasted softly with her creamy skin. She narrowed her eyes, smoothing her hand over her flat abdomen, then up to her full breasts.

Beneath the silk of her bra, her nipples peaked, making the small gold ring that pierced her left one weigh erotically on the sensitive tip. Between her thighs, a matching ring pierced the hood of her clit, and the weight there was driving her insane with the added sensation of pleasure.

She was wet, so slick and hot she could barely stand it. The silk of her thong was damp with need, the roughened texture against her bare cunt lips stroking her arousal higher.

Damn, the waxing Tally had talked her into had hurt like hell the first time. But as her friend had predicted, each session was less painful. The rewards had been amazing. She loved being bare. Loved the lift it gave to her sexual confidence. The amazing sense of freedom and added sensitivity had helped heal a part of her wounded pride after Thomas's death.

Not that another man had touched her there. Until now, she hadn't found the courage to break free of her own fears and try. If Jesse found her wanting, it would destroy her. But she needed to know. Needed to find out if she was woman enough to hold the arrogant, charismatic sexuality of the man who had fascinated her for years.

She knew what he would eventually want. Knew from her own dreams, her own fantasies that she was nearing the point of no control where they were concerned. She stared herself in the eye through the glass of the mirror. Was she perverted? Depraved? She had felt she was, years before, when she first learned of the Trojans and their sexual practices.

When she had first learned she was so in lust and in love with one of the group's major players that she had known she could and would, if he asked, join in his games.

She bit her lip, fighting her own fears and the morals she had been taught in her youth. Hell, she had broken every rule her mother had tried to drum into her head concerning sex and her body. Why should this one be any different? If he loved her...

"Oh God. I've lost my mind." She threw herself on the bed.

She knew Jesse cared for her. He had to. He had taken care of her for almost three years. Had listened to her rage and cry during those first days when the guilt of Thomas's death had weighed on her soul. He had held her, holding back his desire for her, and she knew he had wanted her. There was no hiding the erection that had filled his pants those nights.

He had never given so much time to any other woman. Hell, other than Tess, she knew he hadn't been with another woman in ages. When she asked him about it, he had shrugged and claimed his workload was getting in the way. But he was spending plenty of time with her. Time that he could have used playing. If he had wanted to.

She loved him. She always had. Knew she did. But could she do this? Could she seduce him?

She turned her head, looking at the dress she had laid out on her bed earlier. It was sexy without being crude. The black silk would cling to her curves, without being overtly blatant. The scalloped neckline skimmed the tops of her breasts. The skirt stopped just above her knees. The matching black heels were high, and utterly feminine.

A "dress for success, knock 'em dead" outfit just right for stepping into the offices of Delacourte Electronics and seducing one of the vice presidents in charge. And she had the perfect reason for going in. The letter that had arrived that morning in the mail. Yet another of Thomas's hidden debts.

She drew in a hard, courage-gathering breath before moving from the bed and picking up the dress. She finished dressing quickly, knowing her bravery was waning. Thomas's taunts drifted through her mind as she pulled the material over her head.

Her breasts were too large, he had said. She smoothed her hands over the full mounds. The size C cups of her bra held the flesh securely. Not that she sagged. At least not yet. They were firm and full, but Jesse had large hands. She closed her eyes in pleasure at the thought. And he liked looking at her breasts…hell, he did it often. And his looks were always heated and filled with lust.

She wasn't very tall. Another of Thomas's complaints. She never got wet enough, never acted sexual enough. God, she was so wet now she felt as though she was going to drown in her own desire.

He was wrong. She brushed her hair quickly, watching the silken strands as they curled around her shoulders in a fall of red gold. Not much makeup. She didn't need a lot, and rarely wore it. She didn't want to come off as seductive, but she wanted to seduce.

She was lotioned, waxed and scented from head to toe. Dressed and ready and shaking with nerves two hours later when she walked into Jesse's outer office. Tally's head raised, her brown eyes widening just a bit as a smirk crossed her lips. Terrie prayed she wasn't blushing.

"Should I take my lunch break now?" the secretary drawled in amusement as she sat back in her chair and watched Terrie walk across the room.

Terrie swallowed tightly. "Quick, tell me again what Thomas was?"

Tally frowned. "A walking dick?" she asked as she watched Terrie closely. "Don't tell me you're going after big brother now? Come on, Terrie." She rolled her eyes mockingly.

"He's a walking time bomb. When he gets hold of you he won't let go."

Terrie blew out a relieved breath. "Well, at least you didn't call him a walking dick."

Tally laughed, though the sound was quiet, and filled with amusement. "A walking hard-on, but that can at least be useful."

"Is he alone?" She nodded to the closed door.

Tally looked at the door as she rose to her feet. "Alone and pouting, I think." She grinned as she picked up the pretty purse sitting on her desktop. "And I'm ready for lunch now. Go on in. Tell him I'll see him tomorrow."

Terrie winced. "Long lunch, Tally. He's going to fire you."

The other woman snorted. "I can only get so lucky. Keep him occupied and he'll never miss me." She winked suggestively as she breezed out of the room.

Terrie was left standing, more or less deserted, in the middle of the room. Damn Tally. The least she could have done was stick around to save her if things got too hot.

"Tally, where the hell is that cost estimate..." Jesse threw open his door and stared at Terrie in surprise. "Where the hell did she go this time?"

"Lunch?" Terrie wasn't about to mention the fact that his secretary wouldn't return until the next morning.

He bit off a curse then his eyes narrowed on her. He took in the black dress, the heels, and Terrie watched in fascination as sensuality filled his expression. He went from handsome, darkly dangerous, to sexual pirate within seconds. She fought to still the trembling in her legs as she lifted her hand, flashing the envelope she carried.

He frowned. "Another one?"

Terrie shrugged. "It's not as bad as the others, but I'll need your lawyers to set up the payments..."

He snorted. "Come in here. I'm not going to discuss this standing up."

He turned and disappeared back into his office. Terrie followed slowly.

When she entered the large room, she glanced at the seating arrangement in the corner. He was sitting on one end of the leather couch there, closing out whatever he had been working on in the laptop before pushing it back.

"Sit down." He motioned beside him as he watched her walk to him.

The dark intensity in his green eyes hadn't changed. He looked ready to fuck, and Terrie was suddenly more nervous than she could ever remember being in her life.

She sat perched at the edge of the couch, handing him the envelope carefully.

"If you could just get the payment schedule set up…"

"I'm sure you have enough to cover it." He took the envelope from her and pulled the legal paper from inside. "Thomas was stupid but I wasn't. His shares in the company are safe, Terrie."

Those shares had kept her solvent despite Thomas's death and how quickly he had emptied out both their accounts during their marriage. Jesse had never traced the money, but at least she hadn't suffered in the theft.

Silence filled the room for long moments as he read the letter.

"Stupid bastard," he muttered as he threw the paper to the table. "He's lucky he died. I would have killed him myself by now. Don't worry about it. I'll have the accountant take care of it tomorrow."

"Should I watch my spending for a while?" she asked him carefully. "I don't want to cause any added problems, Jesse."

His mouth tilted with a small grin. "I've invested your money wisely, Terrie. You're fine. Stop worrying."

She wondered if he ever got tired of taking care of her. From the moment news had come that Thomas had died in the car wreck, Jesse had been there. He had taken care of the burial, the horrendous news of the mounting debts. Everything. And he had been taking care of her ever since.

She smiled back nervously, wondering what the hell she was supposed to do now? How did you seduce a man like Jesse? He would give her anything, she knew, but at what cost to himself? How could she be certain she was what he wanted? That he could love her?

"Going somewhere?" He flicked a look at her dress-covered breasts. It was a heated, brooding look, a stroke of carnal interest.

She shrugged nervously. "I thought I'd go to the club today for lunch."

"Stay away from Conover, Terrie," he warned her softly as he turned to her, his eyes blazing with irritation. God, was it jealousy? "I'm telling you, you don't want to push me on this."

Her eyes widened in surprise a second before she frowned back at him. His gaze had narrowed, sensuality vying with a dominant glitter that made her stomach tighten with nerves.

"I didn't mention his name, Jesse."

"You and I both know he's likely to be there," he said. "You're playing with fire. I let you run from me once, Terrie. I won't let you do it again."

She wanted to gape at him. Once again he was making very little sense. "Jesse, I had no intentions of seeing Conover today or ever. It's not my fault you gave him the impression he could help you screw me. And for that matter, what gave you that impression?"

She was angry now. She could feel her veins throbbing with the pulse of blood, the heat that filled her face.

"You're pushing me again, Terrie," he growled. "It's not wise to bait hungry men, baby. Keep it up and you may get more than you bargained for, and we both know you're not ready for that."

She was ready for him. She was ready to take her life back and find the happiness she had denied herself for so long.

"Ready for what?" she snapped back, her fists clenching now. "Ready to be touched? To be a woman for a change? Sorry, Jesse, you're way off base there. I'm more than ready for that. Too bad you're not."

She moved to jump from the couch, to leave the office, to stomp home and scream and curse him as she had more times than she could count already. Unfortunately, Jesse didn't seem ready to let her leave.

Before she could do more than gasp, his arm hooked around her, turning her before he pressed her into the cushions of the couch. The dress rode up her thighs as she stared up at him in surprise and he wasn't helping much as he pressed one hard thigh between hers.

"Oh, Terrie," he said, his voice soft, filled with dark longing. "I'm more than ready for you to be a woman. But are you really ready to be *my* woman?"

He didn't give her a chance to answer. His lips came down on hers in a kiss that sizzled Terrie from her head to her toes. Her hands clenched his shoulders as she fought to keep her senses from reeling, but there was no escaping the firestorm he ignited inside her.

His big hands framed her face, pushing into her hair, holding her still as his tongue invaded her mouth with decadent hunger. It swirled around her own, tempting her, teasing her as it stroked in and out, mimicking a much more earthy, sexual act.

She arched in his arms, helpless now, gorging herself on the pleasure his lips and tongue bestowed as he dominated the kiss. His head tilted, his lips slanting against hers as he groaned deeply into her mouth and one hand moved to cup the fullness of her breast.

Terrie stilled. Was she too large, as Thomas had sworn?

Before the thought was finished Jesse had lowered the zipper in the back of the dress, drawing it slowly down her shoulders as his lips moved to her neck, his breathing rough, heavy, as he began to blaze a path to her right breast.

"Jesse," she whispered his name as she fought to breathe. The sensations rocking through her body were intense, mind destroying, and he hadn't even truly done anything yet.

"Damn." He paused at the cup of her bra, breathing hard and heavy as he so obviously fought for a control she didn't want him to hold onto. "Terrie. Not like this," he whispered, but his fingers stroked over her nipple, causing her to arch in exquisite need.

"Why?" Fear beat at her with razor-sharp talons. "What did I do wrong, Jesse?"

His head rose slowly. The look on his face had her thighs clenching, her vagina spilling more of its liquid heat in a primal demand. His cheeks were sensually flushed, his eyes a brilliant dark green and as hot as lust itself.

"You do too many things right." He tried to laugh, but it sounded more like a strained groan, Terrie thought.

His gaze went to the flesh of her upper breast, his fingers stroking over it almost regretfully as he looked back up at her.

"You know what will happen," he whispered. "I don't want to hurt you, Terrie. I care too much for you to ever want to hurt you. But you know what I'll want."

"And only your wants matter?" she asked him.

He shook his head as he moved away from her quickly, as though if he didn't do it then, he never would. She sat up more slowly, watching as he stared down at her, breathing hard, heavy.

"No, Terrie, that's not all that matters," he informed her impatiently. "If it were, then I'd be in your bed now instead of fighting an erection that never seems to go away."

Her gaze flickered to his hips. She fought to breathe. Nope, there was no hiding that. It was thick and long, pressing demandingly against his slacks.

"Dammit, you should at least act scared," he growled as he sat down carefully in the large chair across from the couch.

"I'm not frightened of you, Jesse." She allowed a smile to tilt her lips as she straightened her dress then reached back to pull the zipper back into place.

She was very much aware of Jesse watching every move she made as she arched to grip the small tab and draw it up slowly.

"Could you handle it?" he asked, and she knew he wasn't talking about the zipper.

She stood to her feet, smoothed her dress down then looked at him coolly.

"Could you?" She arched a brow in question.

He smiled slowly. "Don't dare me, Terrie."

She lifted her shoulder in unconcern. "Don't push me, Jesse. I want you, not a pack of hound dogs. Take that however you want to. And decide which one you want the most. You can let me know when you figure it out."

So much for seduction, she thought sarcastically.

He stood slowly to his feet. "What the hell do you mean by that?" he growled.

"I mean, Jesse, when you decide you want me without all the dire warnings and predictions, then you can let me know. I care about you, as you well know. If I didn't, then I'd be damned if I would put up with your arrogance, or your habit of showing up at my home before sunrise for coffee. The question is, can you do without your buddies long enough to take it?"

She didn't give him time to answer. She swept out of the office quickly, fighting the shuddering need racing through her body, and the sudden tightening of Jesse's muscles as though preparing to move for her. If he wanted her, then he knew where he could find her. Alone.

Chapter Three

ꟃ

He found her asleep on the couch. This was where Terrie slept most of her nights away, curled beneath a light blanket, staring up at the skylight above her. As far as Jesse knew, she hadn't slept in a bed since she had moved from Thomas's years before. Before his death. Before the truth of his abuse had come to light. And Jesse wouldn't have known if he hadn't spent that first week after his brother's death with her.

Her nightmares had humiliated her, he remembered. They had shocked him to the very core of his being. He had known Thomas was different. Had known his brother possessed a cold, cruel side, but he had never suspected the habitual threats he had nearly destroyed Terrie with. So much so that she had been in the process of a divorce when he died. It amazed Jesse that she hadn't killed Thomas herself.

He knelt by the couch, watching her sleep. The blanket covered only her breasts and hips, leaving her long legs bare. She was as naked as sin, lying on her back, breathing deeply as she dreamed. A large man's shirt was pooled on the floor beside the couch as though she had dropped it, unheeded, before lying down. The fragile light of the first rays of morning touched her delicate, honey gold skin, giving it a soft, luminescent color.

She was more beautiful now than she had been dressed in silk and lace at Ella's wedding. And more tempting. Did she, he wondered, know how much she tempted him?

He shook his head. He wasn't a stupid man. He had watched Terrie at that wedding. Watched her expressions, the curiosity in her eyes. She was willing, but uncertain. Needy, but frightened. She was a woman searching for an end to the needs that tormented her, a woman almost willing to reach out.

Almost. His lips quirked into a smile. Terrie couldn't be ordered. She couldn't be persuaded. It had to be her choice. How could he convince her to choose?

Damn. As he stared at her he was amazed once again at what the very sight of her did to him. How it clenched his chest, engorged his cock, had emotions springing to life that he knew he would be much more comfortable without. He didn't need to love this woman. He didn't need to be tormented with her fiery will, her insatiable curiosity and her smart mouth. But there he was. Where he had been since before his brother's death. In love with the one woman he knew he shouldn't want.

He could very well be a fool. He could be making the biggest mistake of his life. He watched her sleep, entranced by her shifting expressions, wondering what dreams filled her head. Was it nightmare or sensual pleasure that had her sighing roughly as she shifted beneath the blanket?

His throat tightened at the thought that nightmares could be visiting her again. That the past could be haunting her with decisions and mistakes not her own. She was too willing to take fault onto her fragile shoulders. Too willing to accept blame when it lay with others.

He lifted his hand, his fingers pushing back a silken strand of red gold hair from her sleep flushed cheek. Her lips parted. Pouty pink curves that he could too well imagine moving beneath his, or enveloping the head of his cock. He grimaced, fighting a groan at the thought of that.

"Terrie?" he whispered her name gently. A soft intimate whisper that he wished he had the right to use. He was taking that right. He was tired of waiting.

The soft moue of her lips at the disturbance had him watching her in amusement. She must have been up late the night before. She shifted again, causing the light blanket to slip further along the full curves of her breasts. Her nipples were peaked, pressing hard against the cloth. On one, the outline of a small gold loop could be seen. The presence of the nipple ring never failed to make his cock jerk in a hungry response. He stared down at it, watching the peaks hardening slowly, becoming engorged as she shivered within whatever dream held her. Sensual pleasure.

"Terrie. Wake up." He spoke louder this time, touching her cheek as her eyes flew open.

She blinked for a second, her gaze drowsy at first as she focused on him. Sensual heat lit her gaze as her lips parted in surprise, her eyes darkening with drowsy sexuality.

"Jesse?" she whispered, her voice husky and dark as she watched him.

She shifted lazily, unaware of the blanket slipping as she did so, the edge catching then falling away from the loop that pierced her nipple. God help him. His whole body tightened. Beaten gold lay against the dark rose areola, looping into the nipple, providing a decadent temptation to his hungry senses. He wondered if she would whimper when he gripped the little loop in his teeth and tugged at it sensually.

"Wake up." He tucked the blanket over the swell of her breasts. Out of sight was not out of mind, though. "We need to talk."

She blinked again. "Talk?"

Her awakening senses were lazy as hell, he knew. Terrie didn't just jump out of the bed. She was like a kitten, drowsy, stretching, accustoming herself to reality before stepping into it.

"Come on, lazybones. Coffee should be ready, and we can talk." He patted her thigh. He wanted to pat something else instead.

She frowned slowly. "I thought I was angry with you?"

Yep, that was his Terrie. Bright-eyed and raring to go.

"You were?" He kept his tone deliberately casual. "Well, you might be madder before the morning's out. Come on, darlin', rise and shine."

He rose to his feet as she thought about that for a minute. She rubbed her eyes then yawned softly behind her hand as she struggled to sit up. He gave her another minute then turned and headed quickly to the kitchen for the coffee.

"Hey," her voice echoed through the house just seconds before she stomped into the kitchen.

He was waiting. He met her at the table, pressed her back into a chair then placed the mug before her. The scent of rich, addicting coffee steamed in temptation beneath the cute little twitch of her nose.

She was still buttoning the overlarge man's shirt that had lain by the couch as she slept. His shirt. His body clenched in reaction at the thought of her lounging around in the shirts he had forgotten here. This one he had used while helping her paint one of the rooms. The paint still stained it.

"You're still in trouble," she muttered as she wrapped her fingers around the mug. "Why the hell are you here anyway?"

Disgruntled, drowsy and clearly remembering exactly why she was angry with him, Jesse thought as he hid his smile. He didn't care much for the welling tenderness that tightened his chest, though. Damn if she couldn't disarm him as quickly as she could arouse him.

"Because you're so cheerful in the morning." He grinned as he carried his own cup to the table and sat down across from her. "My little ray of sunshine."

She shot him a look that was anything but light and uplifting. He hid his smile behind his cup, watching her carefully.

"Cut the crap, Jesse." She pushed her fingers through her hair, sending strands of silk flowing behind her shoulders. "Tell me what the hell you want so I can go back to sleep."

Yep, that was his Terrie. So sweet and gracious she could melt the hardest heart. She had his. Years ago. But it wasn't his heart that needed relief at the moment; it was his cock. Through the long, sleepless night he had come to several decisions where Terrie was concerned. First and foremost being he was tired of waiting. He wanted her with an intensity that bordered on obsession and, by God, he was about to do something about it.

Chapter Four

ഇ

Silence descended between them as Terrie slowly fought her way past the drowsiness that often made it difficult for her to wake up. She was not a morning person. And if she wasn't mistaken, it wasn't much past daylight right now. She could have sworn she had stated her dislike of early mornings.

She finished the first cup of coffee and rose from the table to get another. As she did, she was aware of Jesse coming to his feet as well. He paced to the doorway, sighed, turned back and watched her. She fought to ignore what his look did to her.

"I want to fuck the hell out of you, Terrie."

The smooth, cultured voice broke through the silence of the early morning light and her drowsiness.

Terrie placed the coffee pot back on the counter and fought to still her trembling hands, certain that she couldn't have heard him correctly.

She blinked, staring at Jesse in shock. Despite the confrontation in his office the day before, despite her knowledge that he did want her, she hadn't expected this. Not this soon.

"How very romantic," she snorted, her temper sizzling at his attitude. "Let me just bend over for you now."

Jesse merely watched her coolly, though, with those deep green eyes.

"If you wanted romance, you picked the wrong way to bait me for it," he said as he leaned against the doorway, watching her carefully. "It would be a beneficial arrangement for both of us. And it would sure as hell take care of this frustration we're both fighting tooth and nail. It's stupid to fight something we both want."

She shook her head, aware that her expression must be comical with disbelief. After their confrontation the day before, this was the last thing she had expected.

"Jesse, are you drunk?" she finally asked, narrowing her eyes at him. He had shown up a few times, more than a little relaxed after some party or another he had gone to, but he had never said anything so shocking before and certainly not so early in the morning.

"No, I'm not drunk." He frowned fiercely, his bright green eyes too hot, too dangerously sexy for her peace of mind. "Come on, Terrie. You knew I'd show up after that little dare of yours."

Terrie felt her face flushing. She had expected him, but not this early or this demanding.

She licked her suddenly dry lips nervously, all too aware of how she was dressed now. The large man's shirt covered her okay, but she was completely naked beneath.

"Maybe we should talk about this later." She took a deep breath, fighting for composure. "You know, when you're sane again. And I'm awake."

His frown grew heavier now.

"I'm perfectly sane, just as I'm perfectly aware of how naked you are under that damned shirt, and that fucking nipple ring is driving me crazy. Just as I'm aware of a lot of other things, Terrie. What the hell are you so afraid of anyway? You said you wanted it, now here I am."

Her face flushed. She wondered what he would think of the small ring that pierced the hood of her clit as well. Or the tattoo that stretched across her back. She wasn't nearly as unadventurous as he thought she was. He thought she was too timid, too frightened to accept the things he wanted from her. He had proven that before she met Thomas. And to be honest, she hadn't been certain herself. Hell, she had been terrified at the time. But never once had he had given her the opportunity to try.

Nerves turned to anger at that thought. "I'm not afraid of anything," she said furiously. "But who says I want to have sex with you now? It's not like you're the only man around, Jesse."

Bad question. A sensual smile tipped his lips as his expression took on a brooding carnality that made her cunt clench in arousal. She really wished he wouldn't watch her like that.

"Your nipples are hard," he said softly, his gaze flickering to her breasts.

Her breath caught in her chest. They were hard and aching, just like they always were around him.

"That doesn't mean anything," she told him desperately. "The house is chilly."

"Your pussy is wet." His frank, graphic words had her eyes widening in shock.

"It is not," she lied through her teeth. "Go home, Jesse. I've had enough of this conversation."

But her pussy was wet. Wet and hot and pleading with her to spread her legs and beg him to fuck her. Fuck her hard and deep to relieve the blistering torment of arousal she suffered through. She had to get away from him before she did just that.

"I haven't." He blocked her as she attempted to leave the room.

His tall, leanly muscled body moved in front of her at the last minute, stopping her from reaching the doorway. Terrie stopped; trembling in what she hoped was anger.

"I decided something about this whole situation last night, baby. You're right; you don't need to be warned. You know the facts of my life, and evidently you're willing to chance what's coming. And I've decided something else," he told her softly, maneuvering her until her back came against the wall and his body could press against hers heatedly.

His hands gripped her hips then, his thick, hot erection pressing against her stomach as he moved in closer.

"Like what?" she gasped, her system rioting with heat and arousal.

"Like, maybe you need to be fucked as badly as I need to fuck you," he said softly.

"I'm abstaining," she snapped. "And I'm changing your mind." He pressed his hips against her, and her legs nearly turned to jelly. Oh Lord, his cock was so hard, so hot, even through his slacks.

"You know, Jesse, there's something to be said for seduction. Romance. You remember the concepts. Right?" she reminded him breathlessly. Surely he did. She'd watched him practice it on plenty of other women.

"You want seduction, Terrie? Romance? Show me how it's done, baby. Because right now, all I can think about are the years I've waited to touch you. And I'm damned tired of being patient and waiting."

As was she. But she'd be damned if she would willingly fall at his feet in accordance with his highhanded attitude.

"God. Do you have to be so arrogant? And I've been doing just fine without you so far, so just forget it." Her hands pressed against his powerful chest, but he didn't budge.

"Have you been?" he asked her silkily. "Let me tell you what I want to do to you first, then tell me no."

"I've already heard about your little games," she told him, really angry now. "Do you think Thomas wasn't more than willing to tell me about them?"

Oh yeah, her husband, bastard that he was, had delighted in telling her all about his older brother's sexual exploits. He had taken something he thought Jesse wanted. Had lied to her, tricked her, and had damned near destroyed her life with it.

"I know Thomas told you," he said, his voice gentling, softening in a way that made her ache for him. "Did he offer to let me fuck you, Terrie? Did he tell you how I wanted to tie you down, slap that perfect ass of yours, then fuck it until you screamed? Did he tell you how many times he offered to allow me the chance?"

Shock washed through her body. Months after marrying her, Thomas had refused to touch her, refused to take her in any way. He had accomplished what he wanted. He had taken the woman Jesse had desired, and he never let an opportunity slip by that he didn't remind her of it. Shame coursed over her as she realized he had made Jesse aware of it as well. Had Thomas also told his brother her most betraying secret? The fact that he had overheard her telling Tally how easily she would have given into him? How much she wished she had been given the chance?

"Easy," he whispered as she trembled against him.

"What else?" she finally managed to gasp. "What else did he tell you?"

He frowned. "Was he supposed to tell me something, Terrie?"

She fought to breathe. God, this couldn't be happening.

"Let me go." She pushed against him harder then, too angry to be surprised when he backed up. Then she gasped in shock as he grabbed her arm and hauled her into the living room.

"Dammit, Jesse, stop manhandling me," she ordered him, furious as he spun her around before releasing her.

"Take the shirt off," he growled, his voice darkly dangerous.

Terrie felt her juices begin to coat her cunt lips, her breasts swelling further as his gaze flickered to them once again.

"Jesse, this has gone too far." She restrained the urge to do exactly what he ordered. Damn it, she shouldn't be so turned on with this dominant side of him. Her vagina shouldn't be flaming with arousal, her body desperate to have him touch her.

His hands went to his shirt. She watched, almost whimpering as he quickly pulled it from his trousers and began to unbutton it.

"Take it off, or I'll rip it from you. Which suits me better. When I get you in bed I want you naked, wearing nothing but my touch."

She shuddered, moisture sliding insidiously from her vagina, thick and hot, preparing her.

"What's gotten into you?" she whispered breathlessly as he tore the shirt from his shoulders and dropped it carelessly to the floor.

His eyes were blazing with heat now as he watched her.

"Take the shirt off, Terrie," he rasped out heatedly. "Make me tell you again, and I promise, you won't like the consequences."

"Rape?" she questioned him, though she knew if he touched her, she would fall beneath him willingly.

He smiled. A slow sexy turn of his lips that had her breathing escalating.

"Would it be rape, baby?" he asked her with a slow, knowing drawl. "I don't think it would be. I think your pussy is ready to drip down your leg you're so turned on. I think you need it hard, fast and rough. And I'm more than ready to give it to you."

Terrie felt the blood rush through her system. Lust, hot and addictive, was like a spicy scent in the air, steaming between them. Carnal intent filled Jesse's expression and tightened every line and muscle in his body. Her quick glance to his crotch showed a bulge that made her mouth go dry. Hard, fast and rough. The words had her pussy clenching, drenching her with heated need. He had no idea just how much she did want it, need it, crave it. From him.

His hands reached out, and before she could stop him, he gripped the shirt, wrenching the material until buttons were flying in all directions and she was left bare before his gaze. Gasping, Terrie jerked back from him. Her eyes widened, her body flared with a heat so deep it terrified her.

"Good God." His voice was strangled at he stared at her thighs, the bare folds of her pussy and the gold ring piercing the clit hood. "Son of a bitch, Terrie. Could anything be sexier than that ring? I can't wait to see what it does for you when I get it in my mouth."

Her clit pulsed, her womb clenching with such force it made her breathless, terrifying her with the strength of her arousal. Before she could change her mind she ran. Dodging around him, she sprinted through the room and up the stairs, aware that he had taken off after her.

The breath was sawing desperately through her chest as she scrambled up the steps to the dubious safety of her room. She could lock herself in, run a tub of cold water and immerse herself in it. Surely that would cool the naked lust spearing through her body.

He caught her at the door. One arm manacled her waist as the other slammed the door closed behind them. Jesse held her effortlessly, ignoring her struggles as he tore the shirt from her body then allowed her to wrench out of his arms.

"Bastard!" She turned on him, wishing she were as furious as she was trying to be.

His lips quirked with a smile.

"I'm hearing everything out of your lips but 'no', Terrie," he growled, his hands going to the clasp of his trousers. "Let me hear you say no. Come on, baby, I dare you."

As she stared at him in shock, the rest of his clothes were disposed of. He stood before her gloriously naked, his cock standing out from his body in a hard, thick exclamation of arousal. Terrie's breath caught. He was hard-packed muscle and thick eager lust.

"This is insanity," she gasped, her breasts heaving as his gaze watched the hard-tipped mounds with sexual intensity.

She could feel the weight of the ring in her nipple and her clit, rasping against the sensitivity of each area.

"No, waiting this long was insanity," he growled. "Waiting on you to forget Thomas's stupidity and to see how desperately I've craved you was insanity. I'm about to get real damned smart and do something about it now."

"And if I don't want it?" she questioned desperately. Like that was going to happen in this lifetime.

"Oh, you want it," he told her, stalking closer to her as she backed away from him uneasily. "That pretty, bare cunt of yours is glistening with how bad you want it. And I'm more than happy to give it to you."

She knew he was right, but damn him, he didn't have to be so sure of himself.

"You should wait until it's offered," she said, trying to sneer.

He laughed. A low, deep vibration of humor that speared through her cunt. Oh hell, she thought, she was a goner. She backed away further as he came too close, only to bump against the bed with a gasp. He stopped, inches from her, staring down at her with naked, carnal intent as he reached around her. Her eyes widened as he glanced down at the silk stockings he held in his hand. Stockings she had left there the day before after removing them.

Terrie swallowed tightly. She was afraid to know what was going through his mind at that moment.

"Get on the bed," he ordered her roughly.

Her eyes narrowed on him. The blood was rushing through her system from the chase, the arousal, the forbidden potency of his dominance.

"Make me," she snarled. She wasn't in the mood to submit to anything.

Uh oh. Satisfaction lit his eyes in a blaze of lust so intense it nearly seared her.

"I can," he assured her, his voice dark, sexy. "But you can never go back, Terrie. Once you get a taste of the forbidden, you'll only need more."

And he was forbidden. She stared up at him, sensual terror washing over her in waves. Could she handle him? She had always known she couldn't, so what the hell was she doing here now?

As she watched him, he turned from her abruptly, striding quickly to her dresser. Terrie's eyes widened as he started pulling out drawers, one after the other, until he found what he wanted. The breath left her body when he turned back to her, another pair of her silk stockings gripped in his hand.

She swallowed tightly.

"Get on the bed," he ordered her again.

"Like I said; make me." She braced her body for the struggle to come.

Her cunt was aflame, burning her with need. Sexual intent filled his expression—dark, glittering with purpose as he stared at her, gauging her mood. Then, he smiled again.

Terrie darted away from the bed. She would be damned if she would make it easy for him. But just as she feared, there was little fight involved. His arms came around her, his heavier, muscular body controlling her easily as she struggled against him. She kicked out at him, gasping as her hands went to the hard arms encircling her waist as he wrestled her to the bed.

She cursed; Jesse only chuckled. He threw her to the bed, dodging her fists and her half-hearted kicks as he secured first one wrist then the other to the metal bars of her headboard with soft, silken ties. When he had that accomplished, he moved to her feet.

Terrie kicked at his hands, her body bouncing on the bed as she fought to keep him from securing her feet with the soft stockings before he tied the end to the bed.

When he finished, they were both breathing fast, rough, filling the room with the overwhelming scent of primitive, sexual needs. He stood back from her then, one hand going to his cock, massaging it as he watched her.

"I've dreamed of this," he growled. "Seeing you spread out before me, unable to fight me, unable to deny me."

"Pervert," she snarled.

He chuckled. "Nympho. You love it, Terrie. Your pussy is so hot and wet I swear I think I see steam rising from it."

Chapter Five

ꙮ

Terrie wouldn't doubt it. The heavy, intense ache pulsed in her clit, clenched her womb. She was so horny she felt as though she was going to disintegrate with the need.

He moved to the bed then, lying down beside her, propping his head up with one hand as he watched her. The other smoothed across her abdomen as the muscles there clenched in excitement.

"I've dreamed of this," he told her, his voice soft, throbbing with lust. "Even before that stupid brother of mine fucked up, I dreamed of having you like this. Tied down, your eyes big with excitement and apprehension, the sweet scent of your arousal tempting my senses."

"This won't work, Jesse." Anticipation warred with hesitancy. She had known Jesse was more man than she could handle, that his needs and his tastes could not be satisfied by her.

He liked strong, confident women. Women who could fight him, stand up to him sexually. A partner as tempestuous as he was in bed. Terrie wanted his dominance. She wanted to be made to submit to needs that even she couldn't fantasize of in full detail.

"I think it's working out just fine," he grinned down at her, his hand cupping her breast, his finger tweaking the hard nipple then making her moan helplessly as he tugged at the ring piercing it.

Her breath caught in her throat as the caress speared to her cunt. Intense, fiery, that little pinch of pain nearly had her body exploding in ecstasy.

"Untie me. We'll call it quits here and just forget this ever happened," she gasped as his head lowered to her breast.

He halted, his eyes rising to her.

"Baby, don't take me for a fool," he grinned. "I have you right where I want you. I have no intentions of letting you go now."

Terrie struggled against her bonds, frightened by the arousal that rose inside her as she realized she was well and truly helpless before him. As she watched in dazed fascination, his head lowered further, his tongue reaching out to lick a hard, distended nipple carefully.

"You taste good," he whispered, his lips moving against the hard point, driving her crazy with the need to have him take it into his hot mouth and suckle her strong, deep. "You need clamps for these pretty nipples. Nice and snug. Something that will drive you over the edge with the fire they start."

Her eyes widened. Clamps? Then a sharp, surprised moan issued from her throat as his grip tightened on her nipple, his fingers tugging at the small gold ring there and his teeth worried the other. Just enough pressure to burn with an erotic flame that danced down her spine.

"Like that, baby?" he whispered as his head rose. "A clamp would keep the pressure, make you so crazy that your sweet pussy would gush with your juices. And I'd be there between your thighs, lapping up every delicious drop."

Her hips jerked, a convulsive shudder sweeping through her body at the image he induced. Watching her closely, his gaze went to the flaming curves of her cunt. Terrie watched as his eyes darkened, heated when his fingers met the thick juice that pooled between her spread thighs and coated her bare pussy. They slid through her narrow slit, circled the entrance to her vagina, then continued down to the tightly closed anal opening.

"No." Her shocked whisper had him halting, the tip of his finger stretching her tight entrance erotically.

"No?" he asked her, going no further, tempting her with the forbidden, sensual bite of pain his finger had produced. "I want to fuck you there, Terrie. Not now, not today, but soon. I want to teach you how to prepare yourself for me, how to prepare your body for my cock tunneling into that tight little hole."

She jerked against him, whimpering as the movement of her body forced his finger marginally deeper into her ass.

"Please, Jesse," she whispered, consumed by an arousal, a lust she couldn't hope to control. "I can't stand it."

"What can't you stand, baby?" he asked her with immeasurable tenderness as his finger retreated. "The thought of it, or the building need the thought of it produces?"

She whimpered, shaking her head, unable to answer the question. She didn't know.

"Did Thomas tell you everything about me, Terrie? During the time you were married, did he tell you the rumors of what I like, what I want?"

A woman confident enough to be as dominant as he was sexually. Oh yeah, Thomas had told her often how she could never measure up to what Jesse would need. She almost suspected that he knew how she had lusted for Jesse. The year she had been married to him had been hell.

As her gaze flickered away from his in indecision, his fingers tightened on her nipple, causing her to gasp, her body to jerk with the hot flare of sexual intensity it induced. Her gaze flew back to him.

"Good." He rewarded her with a slow, heated lick to her nipple. "That's what I want in this bed, Terrie. Obedience. No matter what I ask, no matter what I need."

She blinked up him, surprised by his declaration.

"You didn't know?" He smiled that sexy, dangerous smile she loved so well. "Oh yeah, baby. I want you submitting to me in every way, in every position imaginable. I want you screaming because you need me so damned bad. I want you needing this, as much as I need to give it." Before she knew his intent, his open hand delivered a heated slap to her bare, damp cunt.

Terrie was shocked, frightened by a sharp, lust-born moan of pleasure that escaped her throat as the stinging blow vibrated through her body.

"Jesse..." She couldn't say no, though she sure as hell didn't know if she could bear it.

"Like that, baby?" he asked sensually as his hand raised again.

Terrie watched now, her eyes wide, dazed as the hand fell.

"Oh God..." She jerked when the heat came, delivered directly over her pulsing clit, throwing it into shocked, dangerous need.

Her breath caught at the warning flare of release from the blow. Why was he doing this? Was he taunting her? Mocking her shameful needs in some way?

"God, look at you," he growled, lust thickening his voice as he stared down at her in suspended pleasure. "You're flushed and aroused, your expression so confused, so filled with need. You like it don't you, baby? I knew you would."

Another blow landed, burning her, causing her hips to jerk in response, and her juices to slide furiously from her vagina as her clit swelled in response to the sharp pleasure/pain. She was going to orgasm. Oh God, if he smacked her like that just one more time...

She exploded when the blow fell again. Her cunt flamed from the sensual pain, her vagina pulsing as her clit exploded in a firestorm of destructive heat. It raced up her spine, through her womb, shuddering through her body, flaming through her veins as she cried out in shameful pleasure.

"Yes," his voice growled from a distance. "Oh hell, Terrie, I can't wait."

He moved over her body then as his lips lowered to hers. She took his kiss and fought for more. Her lips opened for his tongue, hers twining with it, stroking, tasting the heat of his mouth as he moved between her thighs. His hands weren't still either. They cupped her breasts, tweaked her nipples with heated pressure and had her hanging on an edge of such desperate pleasure she wondered if she would survive it.

She was bucking against his body, twisting closer, needing more of his heat, his carnal promise. Lust was like a demon that possessed her now, filled her with erotic images, destroying her body with the sensual pleasure washing over it.

Finally, he tore his lips from hers, staring down at her, his eyes almost black with emotion and lust as she felt the broad head of his erection touch her slick, cream-coated cunt.

Terrie stilled, her arms straining at her bonds as she watched him in anticipation.

"Slow and easy first," he growled.

He pressed against the soft folds of her pussy, the broad head of his cock parting them, sliding against them as he paused at her vaginal entrance. He was hot and thick, tempting her, teasing her with the invasion to come. His hand reached down, moving his shaft against the sensitive flesh, running it through the thick cream that coated her.

"Jesse." She couldn't halt the plea that escaped her lips.

He didn't answer her, but she felt her breath whoosh from her throat as his cock nudged into the entrance. She could feel him parting her, stretching her already. It had been so long since she had known the touch of a man. She hadn't had sex with Thomas since just a few months after their marriage. She knew she would be tight, and his cock was broad, and more than willing to stretch the sensitive tissue there.

He pressed in tighter, retreated, then worked the head of his shaft into her again. He repeated the sensual movements, parting her greedy flesh, stretching her as she groaned and arched into the invasion.

"So hot and tight," he whispered. "I want to enjoy each minute it takes to work my cock into you to the hilt, Terrie." His words had her cunt clenching on the bulging head of his erection. "Oh yeah, baby, clench that sweet cunt on me. Fight it. Make it better, Terrie. So much better."

His expression was a tight grimace of pleasure as he worked against the further tightening. She did as he bid, tightening on him, milking his cock as he worked another inch inside her. It was the most erotic act she had ever endured. Fighting the invasion of his hot lance as he forced his way in further.

Her hips jerked, bucked, her pussy rained its moisture over him, heating them, creating a gliding friction that was making her insane. His hands tightened on her hips, his muscles tightening as she watched through eyes half closed. His control was slipping. She could feel it. She tightened her muscles on him again, straining to force him out when everything inside her wanted him deeper.

The sensual lash of heated pressure inside her vagina was killing her. A sharp burning bite as he pressed in deeper, not even half his cock had worked its way inside her. Her thighs strained as she fought the entrance, her cries whispering past her throat now as the pleasure rocked her body.

His hands clenched on her hips, perspiration glistening on his flesh as he gritted his teeth. She rolled her hips against the hard, straining penis that rocked inside her.

Her scream shattered the thick, sensually charged atmosphere as his control snapped. He thrust hard and heavy inside her, burying his cock to the hilt as her muscles quivered around him, tightened and fought to accept the broad length suddenly filling it.

Terrie felt the warning tremors of her climax pulsing in her vagina. The hot, hard burn, the pinch of pain. The flaring intensity of the pleasure was too much for her body to fight against. The hard, milking contractions on his cock were too much for Jesse to fight.

His elbows were braced at her shoulders as his hips began to move. His shaft retreated, only to return in a heavy, invading thrust that had her arching to him, twisting against him. Her body was no longer her own, but was controlled only by the hard, driving thrusts that rocked her, filled her world with a pleasure she knew would destroy her.

Deep, penetrating, stretching her to her limits, his cock thrust in and out, driving her to a pinnacle of such unbelievable pleasure she was screaming out for her release. Fire assailed her quaking pussy, tightened it, milked his cock until she exploded with such intensity that she couldn't breathe, couldn't fight the mind-boggling sensations as her orgasm raced through her body.

She was distantly aware of Jesse lunging powerfully inside her again and again, then his cry joined hers. She felt another rippling climax tear through her as she felt the hot, hard blasts of his semen spurting inside her gripping flesh.

His lips were at her neck, caressing her flesh, hard male growls of pleasure echoing in her ears as he shuddered over her. Pulsing mini-explosions rippled over her body, through her cunt, as she trembled through the last of her powerful climax.

She was gasping for breath now, her flesh sensitized, covered with an invisible film of ultra-sensitive nerve endings that caused her body to shudder with each ragged breath that pressed her tighter against him. Weak, spent, she collapsed long moments later, dazed and uncertain as she never had been in her life.

Chapter Six

ꩠ

What had he done? Jesse lifted himself from Terrie's spent, damp body and moved gingerly to her side as he stared down at her. Her eyes were closed, her breathing still hard, heavy. The little gold ring at her nipple trembled as she shuddered again.

Jesse sighed in self-disgust as he moved to release her from the silken bonds he had tied her with. He had lost his mind and his control, something he had never done before. The minute he had seen her eyes flash with heat, her nipples poking against his shirt, all common sense had fled. He had taken her with few preliminaries. So intent on sinking his cock inside her that nothing else had mattered.

He had broken one of his own strongest rules. Complete agreement. Complete surrender and submission from her. Complete control from him. He had taken her hard, hot, without control, reveling in her heated struggles and the hot lust in her eyes.

She didn't move as he released her, but her eyes opened the barest bit as she watched him untie her feet. He kept a careful eye on those feet. They could be lethal when she was pissed. And she had every reason to be pissed.

"So what now?" He stared down at her, wondering if, despite the pleasure, he had just made the biggest mistake of his life.

She arched her brow. The slow, deliberately mocking move had him carefully hiding a wince. He moved back from the end of the bed carefully as her legs shifted lazily.

"You have got to be the least romantic man I have ever laid my eyes on," she sighed. "Don't you have to go to work or something? I want to sleep."

He cleared his throat. "I took the morning off."

"Why?" She frowned at him. Jesse had a feeling she was well aware of the fact that he was trying to figure out just how pissed she was. She was deliberately keeping her expression only mildly curious, giving him no hint to her feelings.

His gaze flickered over her nude body. The delicate rings piercing her flesh entranced him. Only then did he notice the one piercing the skin of her belly button as well.

"When in the hell did you get those piercings done?" He fought the need to cover her body and take her again, then and there.

His cock was so hard it pulsed in agony.

"About a month after I got the tattoo." She shrugged carelessly.

His eyes went over her body again. He didn't see a tattoo.

"What tattoo?" He was instantly wary of the wicked glint in her eyes.

She turned over, slowly. His eyes widened. It stretched across her back. A delicate intricate vine and two graceful, open flowers just above the full globes of her buttocks.

"Do you like?" She turned her head, flexing the muscles of her ass temptingly.

Jesse felt perspiration dot his forehead. His cock was screaming for action, his hands itching to clench those tight little globes, to separate them. He shook his head, fighting for control.

"Why?" he finally asked as he fought to breathe.

She turned back over, watching him carefully.

"Tally dared me."

He shook his head, his gaze now centered on the glistening ring at her clit. He moved closer to the bed, his mouth watering, the need to taste her nearly overwhelming.

"Tally?" he asked, wondering what the hell his secretary could have to do with this.

"Yes. Tally. Tally Raines." The name slid through his mind with dawning horror. "We've been friends forever."

He nearly lost his erection. "She's evil," he burst out, shaking his head as he thought of the wily, sarcastic-tongued little shrew that ruled the offices at Delacourte Electronics.

"Evil?" She tilted her head, smirking at him. "You're just mad because she doesn't kiss your ass and makes you do your own filing."

He was not going to spend the rest of the morning arguing over the sharp-tongued dragon he had made the mistake of hiring last year. As soon as possible, she would be transferring to another office anyway. He'd be damned if he would have someone in his office who could out-yell him. And damned if she couldn't do it.

"Stay away from Tally," he growled. "She's dangerous."

He picked up his clothes, dressing quickly. If he didn't get out of the bedroom he was going to lose control again. He had to figure out what the hell had happened to his control before he even considered touching her again.

She lay there on the bed. Calm. Cool. Her hazel eyes quizzical as she watched him pull his clothes on. She didn't say anything, and he'd be damned if he knew what to say at this point.

"I'll call you this evening," he said as he tucked his shirt into his pants, glancing at her, his temper building as she watched him so calmly. She should be furious. Screaming, cursing and threatening him until hell wouldn't have him.

"Don't bother." She finally shrugged. "I wasn't looking for anything, Jesse. You started this, if you'll remember. Not me."

"Like hell I did," he snapped as he strode back to the bed and pulled her from it as she gasped in surprise.

He had her in his arms, her gaze widening, her perfect lips parting on a gasp.

"Jesse," she cried out, arousal and surprise vying in her voice.

"You started this the other night, Terrie," he reminded her brutally as he fought the lust pounding through his veins. "I told you not to push me. Not to provoke something you couldn't handle. Now I would suggest, for the time being, you stop pushing or we may both come to regret it."

Before she could let loose with the fury of words he could see building in her expression, his lips slammed down on hers, parting them. Her tongue meeting his halfway as he pushed it past the seam of her lips. He groaned, arching her closer into his body as he ate at her, licking at her, savoring the taste of her.

They were both breathing hard when he pulled back. He knew he was damned near as dazed as she looked and once again his body shuddered as he fought for control.

"Tonight." He was breathing hard as he set her carefully away from him. "I'll call you tonight."

He left the room before he lost all sanity. He was within seconds of throwing her back to the bed and fucking her again with a driving hunger he felt would never be sated. A hunger he had never known for another woman.

Chapter Seven

ꩡ

"Tally, hold all calls. I'm unavailable until after lunch." Jesse entered the outer office, his eyes narrowing on the sardonic expression his secretary held.

Tally Raines was an unholy terror as far as he was concerned. The curvy, haughtily aloof Filipino watched him with what he was terribly certain was a knowing expression.

"I'll be sure to do that," she drawled, her cultured voice filled with amused patience. "Would you like coffee, sir?"

He paused at his office door and glanced back at her, his eyes narrowing as she watched him with superior female indulgence.

"Coffee, please," he said coolly. "Then get me the Conover contract so I can go over it before sending it to James."

"It's on your desk." She rose gracefully from her chair, long black hair rippling down the back of her white silk blouse to touch her shapely hips. "Anything else?"

Yeah, no more body piercings for Terrie, he thought with a flash of temper that he tamped down. Dammit, the woman was a menace.

"Nothing else," he finally growled. "Bring the coffee as soon as possible."

"Of course." She sounded mildly surprised that he would think she would delay.

Jesse figured he might get the coffee before he left the office that evening. He grunted rudely, jerking the door open, and entered his own office. Now he knew why she drove him crazy. Terrie had to be giving her lessons.

He grimaced as he took his seat behind his desk and flipped open the file waiting on him. Lucian Conover was an old friend; part of the exclusive group that had begun back in college. Not that any of them had been moronic enough to name the group. He did know he had broken one of the cardinal rules, though. Control. Complete control. Only her pleasure mattered. Only her complete, mindless surrender to the pleasure was the goal. Not his.

He pushed his fingers wearily through his hair, frowning down at the papers before him as he fought to make sense of what had happened. Fought to try to at least understand how he had managed to land himself in this predicament. Never in his entire adult life, certainly not since admitting to himself the extreme pleasure he gained from his sexual lifestyle, had he lost control like this.

"Oh dear. Did you find a problem with the contracts?" Tally's smooth voice cut through his musings as she set the steaming cup of coffee at the side of the desk.

"Contracts are fine." He lifted the edge of the paper he was staring down at. "Thank you for the coffee, Tally. I'll call you if I need you."

"You have messages." Her voice was insistent.

Jesse lifted his head, turning it until he could gaze up at her with level patience. Dealing with Tally demanded patience.

Her dark brown eyes danced with amusement, her lips tilting into a smirk that had him narrowing his eyes in suspicion.

"What?" he asked her carefully.

"Messages." She laid the papers beside the cup of coffee, still watching him, the smirk firmly in place.

"Thank you," he growled. "You can go now, Tally."

She sighed with exaggerated patience. "Very well. But might I suggest a shower, Mr. Wyman? The smell of sex is lingering. And since some of us are doing without at the present, we don't like being reminded."

She sauntered from the room. Jesse watched her leave, restraining the urge to bare his teeth in temperamental frustration. Dammit. He leaned back in the chair heavily, closing his eyes, fighting his need to stalk from the office and return to the object of his frustration. He knew years ago Terrie would drive him insane. She was now proving his fears as fact. And his cock was proving to be a very willing sacrifice to breakdown. Even now it throbbed in demand, in explicit, mounting excitement at the thought of touching her again.

Control. His jaw clenched as he fought for it. Control. His fist tightened as he returned to the file. Son of a bitch. He sighed wearily as the words blurred and once again he fought to understand his own weakness.

* * * * *

"Oh Terrie, you are such a bad girl." Tally stepped into the house as Terrie stood back and welcomed her in.

Her brown eyes, usually cool and mocking, were filled with warmth and humor as Terrie shook her head wearily.

"I know he didn't tell you. By the way, he thinks you're evil," Terrie informed her as she closed the door and led the way into the living room. "So how did you figure it out?"

"Hmm," Tally mused. "It could have been the lingering smell of sex, and Giorgio's Red was unmistakable. He should have showered before coming in," she pouted. "I haven't had sex in months, Terrie. I don't like being reminded."

Terrie flushed, though she couldn't help the laughter that welled from her lips.

"I'll be sure to let him know," she promised her friend lightly.

Tally shrugged. "No problem, dear, I already have." She sat down in the high-backed chair across from the couch and lifted a dark brow curiously. "Now come, give Tally all the dirty details. Was he positively sinful?"

Terrie collapsed back on the couch.

"He was sinful," she sighed. "And very upset for some reason."

She couldn't get his reaction out of her mind. It was unlike Jesse to appear less than confident. Yet, for some reason, that impression had nagged at her brain. As though something about the act had bothered him more than he let on.

"Hmm. Yes, he was quite out of sorts when he came into the office," Tally laughed in sheer delight. "You should have seen him trying to pretend to read that contract he had in front of him. But his expression was just dazed. I loved it."

Terrie shook her head at her friend, but couldn't hold her own laughter back. There was no one as dryly mocking as Tally could be. Her amusement and general outlook on life never failed to keep Terrie laughing.

"I don't know what to do now, Tally," she finally sighed as she leaned back on the couch. "Do you think I didn't please him?" It was her biggest fear.

"Darling, you blew his ever-loving mind," Tally chuckled. "His nerves are fried, his preconceived notions have flown out the window, and the man is scrambling to figure out what the hell happened. I would say you were the best he's ever had."

Terrie bit her lip. Yeah, he seemed pretty damned confused when he rushed from the bedroom.

"You know what he'll do next," Tally warned her. "If he brings Lucian with him, at least videotape it so I can watch."

Terrie's eyes widened. "Videotape?" she gasped. "No way."

"Oh, come on." Tally waved her hand negligently. "At least I'm not asking to participate."

Terrie stilled, then blinked. The object was to throw Jesse into overload. To show him she could meet him more than halfway. What if she… It would never work. Would it?

"What are you up to?" Tally asked her, laughter heavy in her voice. "Oh, I just love it when you plot. You're almost as good as I am."

She watched her friend closely. Was Tally really as adventurous as she swore she was?

"Participation," Terrie whispered. "Turning the tables on Jesse."

Tally's eyes widened in surprise. "Oh Terrie," she exclaimed gleefully. "You're learning. You're learning. Tell me what you're planning."

"Jesse likes to share his women." Terrie fought the racing of her heart. "What if I sort of share Jesse? What would he do?"

Tally was obviously shocked. "Share him?" she said slowly. "How?"

"You know." She lifted her brows suggestively, leaning forward. "I'll tie him down, somehow. Like he did me. Then you can…"

"Me?" Tally questioned with mocking surprise. "Hold up here. We never said me, Terrie. Jesse is not my type."

"Neither is Lucian, but I notice you can't help but pant around him. Come on, Tally. Who else could I trust?" she pleaded. "I don't want you to fuck him. Just help me torture him. That's all. I swear."

"Just torture him?" She lifted her eyebrows consideringly. "Nothing else. Right?"

"No way. Nothing else." Terrie could never tolerate anything else.

Tally smirked. Her fingernails tapped out a fierce little rhythm on the arms of the chair as she watched Terrie closely. "When?"

Terrie swallowed nervously. "I don't know. Soon."

Terrie watched the cool, almost feline look that crossed her friend's face. "This weekend. I need time to prepare," Tally sighed. "These things must be planned, Terrie. Until then, you can drive him insane some more. Keep doing things that throw him off balance. Give him a blowjob under his desk. That drives those executive types crazy. Don't let him get the best of you. The minute he does, he'll regain control and it will all be over with. Stay in control, Terrie."

"In control." Terrie nodded. God, what the hell was she doing?

Tally rose to her feet. "I'll help, of course." She smiled with slow pleasure and for just a moment, Terrie wondered at the look of gleeful anticipation in her friend's face.

"Tally, you scare me," she sighed, not for the first time. "What are you planning?"

She shrugged her slender shoulders negligently. "Don't worry, sunshine, Auntie Tally will take care of everything." Then she narrowed her eyes. "Do you need another piercing?"

Chapter Eight

ꟹ

Keep him off guard. Keep him off guard. Terrie repeated the words as she breezed through Jesse's outer office the next day. She ignored Tally's, "Go get 'em tiger," and entered the office as though it were her own.

Jesse raised his head from a file and his instant response nearly had her pausing. His eyes darkened as he took in the vee cut, button-down, white silk slip dress and strappy sandals she wore.

"Terrie?" He watched her cautiously as she moved around the desk and stared down at him with a frown.

"You didn't show up for coffee this morning," she reminded him. "And I was up waiting on you. Do you have any idea how hard it is for me to get up at the crack of dawn, Jesse?"

His lips twitched in amusement. "I did call, baby," he told her. "You didn't answer so I left a message."

"Your excuse was flimsy." She propped her hands on her hips, deliberately allowing her breasts to swell above the top of the dress. "Come on, Jesse. You never get up late."

He leaned back in his chair, his eyes riveted on the swelling mounds. "I didn't get to sleep until late." He cleared his throat then swallowed tightly. "I was going to stop by this evening. I know I left the message."

Terrie snorted. She got the message. "Be ready, baby. We have plans," she repeated for him. "I don't think so, Jesse. You just knew that one would work for me," she assured him sarcastically, barely retraining the urge to roll her eyes.

She moved to prop her hip on his desk as Jesse moved to touch her. Her nerves and his movements, combined, had her jostling the nearby penholder and knocking it over. Pens scattered across the desktop.

"Oops." Some of the pens rolled off the desk and she bent to try to retrieve them. "I'll get them," she promised softly, suggestively as two bounced from his knee to the carpet beneath the desk.

* * * * *

Jesse jerked in response as her hand braced on his knee and she bent to retrieve the pens. Damn her, no bra. He drew in a deep breath as her head disappeared under the desk.

"Dammit, Jesse." The office door opened at the same time she worked herself beneath the desk. Lucian Conover walked quickly into the room, the door slamming behind him. "That viperous little shrew working the desk outside swore you weren't even here. I knew that was your car outside."

Jesse stilled. Terrie moved beneath the desk. A sinuous ripple of her body against his leg nearly had him trembling in anticipation.

"I have to work sometime, Lucian." He shrugged as he leaned back in his chair. "What do you need?"

He felt Terrie's hand move up his ankle. God, she wouldn't. He drew in a deep breath, knowing he had never imagined his delicate little temptress daring something this sensual, this quickly.

"I need those cost estimates on that new chip your boys are working on. It was supposed to be in my office yesterday," Lucian sighed as he sat down in one of the plush chairs in front of the desk. "Besides, I wanted to talk to you about that pretty little sister-in-law of yours."

Jesse frowned. Beneath the desk Terrie's hand stilled at his knee for just a second. She shifted silently then and he blinked as he felt her teeth nip the flesh above his knee.

"Go away, Lucian, I'm busy." He fought to keep his voice calm, even.

Her hands were creeping up his thighs, her nails scraping through the silk of his slacks as she neared the engorged length of his cock. Son of a bitch. She was going to do it.

"Oh hell, don't get possessive on me." Lucian frowned. "She's a pretty little thing, Jesse. Don't tell me you haven't fucked her yet."

His belt came free.

"Lucian, Terrie isn't up for discussion," he growled.

The blood was rushing through his body, throbbing in his cock. The thought of fucking Terrie was killing him.

"Dammit, are you stalking her yourself?" the other man questioned impatiently. "Come on, Jesse, she's family."

"Not hardly," Jesse growled as he felt his slacks loosen. Terrie had managed to slide the zipper down without a sound.

He felt perspiration gather on his forehead. This would kill him. Her hands were warm, inquisitive, as they worked the panel at the front of his briefs to free his straining flesh. Damn. He would have a stroke before she ever freed him. The sensation of her fingers moving against his sensitive cock was nearly more than he could bear. Her nails scraped the shaft, sending a firestorm of electrical impulses up his spine as he fought to keep from shuddering in pleasure. Hell, he wished Lucian would just get the hell out of the office.

"Not hardly what?" Lucian frowned. "Not hardly stalking her, or she's not hardly family?"

Her tongue twirled around the head of his erection. He gritted his teeth, his hands clenching on the arms of his chair as the moist caress stole his breath. God, she was killing him.

"Jesse, are you okay?" Lucian frowned. "You're acting damned strange."

"Long day." Jesse fought to keep his voice even, his gaze flickering to his lap where Terrie had laid her head against his thigh, her little pink tongue licking the shaft of his cock like it was some kind of living lollipop.

"Long day?" Lucian's startled question had Jesse staring back up at him, dazed. "Dammit, Jesse, it's barely afternoon."

Jesse moved his hand to Terrie's soft hair, clenching in the silken strands as her mouth covered the bulging head of his erection. Damn it, he was not going to come while he was fighting so hard to hide what she was doing to him. Not that he cared if the other man knew, but he was afraid she did.

"Lucian, let me call you later," he growled as the wet heat of her mouth began to move over the head of his cock. "I'll have the estimates for you then."

Terrie decided that was the time to try to swallow his cock. She suckled him deep and slow, her tongue flickering along the sensitive underside like an erotic whip. At the same time, Lucian's gaze fell to the floor and his eyes widened in surprise at something he obviously glimpsed through the inch-wide crack between the floor and the desk backing.

Lucian sat back in his chair with a wicked grin as Jesse fought to keep from cursing. Hell, he just hoped Lucian didn't decide to ruin it for him. This was the most incredibly sensual thing he had ever experienced.

"So have you decided if you're stalking her or not?" Lucian suddenly asked as he watched Jesse carefully. "Would be good to know before I try to fuck her myself."

"Shut the fuck up, Luc," he cursed roughly. But he felt Terrie shiver. Her mouth tightened on his cock, her tongue stroking him with quick little darts that were driving him crazy.

"Guess you are." Lucian came to his feet reluctantly. "Hell, let me know if you change your mind."

"Don't hold your breath." Jesse was almost panting as Terrie sucked his cock slow and easy. It was the sweetest torture he could imagine.

He ignored Lucian as he left the room, his gaze going to his lap, watching as his cock disappeared in and out of her mouth.

"There you go, baby," he whispered, his voice rough. "Just like that. Suck it slow and easy. Just like I intend to fuck you. Slow and easy, baby."

She slurped on his flesh, a soft moan breaking from her throat as his fingers tightened in her hair.

"Beautiful," he growled, feeling her shudder as he spoke to her. Did she like the words, he wondered? Was that what made her tremble each time he spoke? "You're so pretty, baby, your mouth wrapped around my cock, sucking me."

She moaned deeply as he spoke, her hand going to her own breast, her fingers plucking at her nipple. God, he wanted to do that for her. Wanted to pull at those pretty hard points. Watch them darken, harden further.

"What are you going to do when I come in your mouth, Terrie?" he asked her. "Do you think it's going to be over? Do you think you'll just walk away as though it didn't happen?"

She moaned. The bulging head of his cock was caressed, tortured, as his words spurred her on. Her lips stretched around it, her eyes closed, her expression dazed as she gave him the best blowjob he had known in his life.

"Yeah, suck it harder, baby," he whispered as she began to do just that. "I'll fill your mouth, then I'll fill that tight pussy of yours, Terrie. I'm going to fuck you so hard you'll scream for me."

He was fucking her mouth now. Her hands gripped his cock as she moaned around his flesh, licking him, suckling at him as he fucked her, his cock tightening, throbbing. His hands clenched around the strands of hair he held captive, holding her in place, watching her glistening mouth take him with each stroke.

"I'm going to come, Terrie." He couldn't stand it. His body was alive for a change, his cock so sensitive, so desperate for release he was burning alive. It was one of his greatest fantasies, his greatest needs. Terrie, kneeling before him, moaning for him, her body hot and receptive. God help him, he loved her.

His hips arched, his cock pressing to her throat as he felt his release wash over him. Lightning shot through his scrotum, up his spine, arching his body as the first pulse of his seed shot into her mouth.

"Take it all," he whispered breathlessly as he felt her swallow, felt her tongue dance over the exploding tip as he shot into her mouth again. Then again. And still he was hard. Pulsing. He fucked against her lips, panting for breath before he reached down and dragged her from beneath the desk.

"Bad girl," he accused her softly as she stared at him in surprise. "That was very bad, Terrie. Let's see what kind of punishment we can come up with for you."

"What?" Her eyes widened as he jerked her over his lap, holding her down on his legs as she struggled weakly against him.

Jesse jerked her skirt above her buttocks, grimacing at the sight of the bare globes he revealed.

"Jesse, have you gone crazy? Oh my God!" she sang out as his hand connected sharply with the first rounded curve.

She stilled, her breathing heavy, hard.

"Can you still taste my come in your mouth, baby?" He smoothed his hand over the reddened flesh.

"Yes." Her voice broke when his finger ran down the cleft of her ass.

"Son of a bitch." He paused at the stretched, filled little hole of her rectum. The base of the plug she wore was heated, warm from her body. The ultra-soft, jelly material stretched her ass, filling her, making his cock twitch in jealousy.

He smacked her ass again. She flinched, crying out in startled awareness at the bite of pain.

"From now on, only I can fill your ass." He smacked her again to reinforce the order. "Seduction is over, Terrie. Now the fun begins."

He watched the cheeks of her ass redden as he delivered several more stinging slaps. She writhed beneath him, crying out in pleasure as he spanked her with erotic heat. She was twisting on his lap, her buttocks lifting imploringly when he stilled.

He couldn't resist. He was too weak, he thought. She was supposed to seduce him. He wasn't supposed to be this easy. He pulled the plug free of her anus, watching the stretching of the little hole, his eyes narrowing as she whimpered at the retreating pleasure. Just as slowly he pushed it back into her, feeling her shudder in pleasure.

"I'm going to fuck you, Terrie," he growled. "I'm going to fuck you so hard, so deep, you'll never forget what it's like to have me fill you."

He ripped the small thong from her, tossing the scraps to the floor as he jerked her up then pushed her back on the desk. He spread her legs, moving between them before he paused, his eyes widening as he caught sight of the little hoop framing her swollen clit.

"Son of a bitch." He lost his breath.

Her cunt was perfectly bare, smooth and glistening with her juices. The little bright gold hoop piercing the hood of her clit was so sexy, so erotic he nearly came then and there from the sight of it alone.

He was within seconds of pressing his engorged cock home when a heavy knocking at the office door had them both scrambling away from the desk. Dammit. Why hadn't he had Lucian lock the fucking door?

He hurriedly fixed his slacks, glancing at Terrie as she smoothed the dress nervously over her hips. At least she could hide the damned proof of what nearly happened. He sat down heavily in his chair to hide the telltale tenting of his slacks as the door pushed open.

"Mr. Wyman, Mr. Delacourte needs you upstairs." Tally stepped into the office, her expression perfectly bland as Terrie fidgeted by his side. "He said to tell you they have the Conover chip ready, but there's a problem."

There was a problem all right, and it wasn't with a chip. He glanced from Terrie, back to Tally, then moved carefully from behind the desk. He had talked to Jase hours ago, though he hadn't gone through Tally to do so. That damned chip was fine. What were those two up to?

"I'll see you tonight." He turned to Terrie, watching her carefully.

"Alone, Jesse," she murmured firmly. "Tonight. Alone."

He watched her carefully for long moments. "Alone." He nodded shortly then moved quickly from the office. Damned women. They were up to something. The question was, what?

Chapter Nine

ꟷ

She could pull this off, Terrie assured herself as she prepared the bedroom for Jesse's arrival. She knew they would make it to the bedroom. At least, she hoped they did. She drew in a hard breath, checked her appearance for at least the tenth time, and tried to still her nerves. She had never attempted anything this brave without a drink first. There was something to be said for false courage.

"Stop worrying." Tally moved into the room from the bathroom. "Just get him in here and the rest will work out."

Tally was dressed in form-hugging black. She looked like a cat burglar. Terrie couldn't help but roll her eyes before her nerves got the best of her again.

"What if he doesn't go along with it?" She pushed her fingers restlessly through her hair. "What if he's furious, Tally?"

"Then he can't cry foul when you won't." She shrugged. "Turn about and all that, darling. Besides, Jesse isn't going to be furious. He'll be intrigued at first. Wondering how far you'll go. Won't he be surprised?"

She could tell Tally was trying her best not to crack up with laughter.

"You are finding this much too amusing, Tally," Terrie sighed. "There's no way this is going to work."

She sat down on the bed and shook her head wearily. Why was she doing this? It wasn't the first time she had asked herself this question. She knew, when it came right down to it, that anything Jesse wanted she would give him willingly. She had known it years ago. She knew it now.

She also knew, though, that no one had given to Jesse in the same manner. Through the years she had known him, watched him as he gave unselfishly of himself. Always. To Thomas, it had been money. The only thing Thomas had ever cared about. For his twin, James, it was his support, continually, no matter where or when. It was the same for her, for his friends. Often, no one had to even ask. If Jesse knew there was need, then Jesse gave.

Just giving herself to him didn't seem to be enough. She wanted to give to him in the same ways she knew he would give to her. His pleasure alone. A fantasy she knew he had never had. Dominant, alpha Jesse would have never allowed himself to be tied down, giving his control to two women. That was his territory. He bestowed the pleasure; he never selfishly took. And she had been allowing it for as long as she had known him. She had taken all he gave her, never questioning why, never wondering at his needs. Was it really so bad?

She knew it didn't happen often. That even in Tess and Cole's relationship it had only happened a handful of times. Just as she knew Jesse would never go back to Tess now. What happened, she wondered, as each of the group married? Why, when it was so imperative before the marriage, did that need to share their women ease later in the relationship? At first she had been unaware it did, until Jesse had brought up the subject months before.

I guess that need just isn't there, he had said, shrugging. *Love changes things, Terrie. It changes a lot. But that doesn't mean I wouldn't want the woman I love to know that side of me. Or to miss out on that particular pleasure. It's a part of who I am.*

She hadn't understood it at the time. Hell, she didn't know if she understood it now. Why would it change? And why, as she thought about it, did she want to give Jesse that brand of pleasure herself in a small way? A sexual, intensely erotic gift that there was no way in hell she would ever repeat.

She had thought it was to turn the tables on him. Had convinced herself it was. But it wasn't really. She wanted Jesse to know she accepted him. To know she knew him. To know she understood. And she wanted to give him a gift that she knew no one else ever had.

"Terrie," Tally sighed as she sat down beside her. "Jesse isn't a serious thing for me. But you're my friend. I promise you, when he gets here and we start this, I will take good care of your man and your friendship."

Terrie looked at her friend silently. Tally sighed.

"I don't want Jesse physically, Terrie. You know this. But I know what you want for him. We're friends, and I want your happiness above anything. So I want to help you do this."

Terrie tilted her head, watching the other woman closely. For once, Tally's dark gaze held no mockery, no laughter.

"No wonder Jesse doesn't ever know what to make of you," she whispered softly. "You're like him, Tally. Unselfish…"

Tally snorted as she rose quickly to her feet. "No way, Terrie. I'm very selfish. When we're done, you're helping me get that job at Conover's. Your man is a lousy boss. Hell, he caught onto his own filing as though he's supposed to do it himself," she grunted. "So never fear, it comes with a price."

Terrie hid her smile. She had never known what a true friend she had. But she did now. The nights Tally had forced her out of the house, getting her drunk, tattooed, pierced. Terrie remembered those bleak days clearly. Days when she had fought to make sense of her life, and who she was. Days she had wondered if Thomas had been right. If she was truly less of a woman than she had ever believed. Never enough woman for a man like Jesse.

"Okay, we can do this," she announced. "He'll be here in less than an hour. I'll get him in the handcuffs, but he's going to be pissed."

"Of course he will." Tally smiled. "That's the best part." She rubbed her hands together with mocking eagerness. "Can we blindfold him?"

Chapter Ten

ઈ

Terrie was waiting for Jesse when he stepped slowly into the bedroom. The house was dark, lit only by the candles that showed the way from the front door, up the stairs and into her room. The bedroom was lit by dozens of the small scented candles, casting his expression in shadow. But she caught a glimpse of his somber expression as he stepped into the room.

Tally was waiting on the screened-in back porch, watching for the bedroom light to flicker. The sign that she could enter. What Terrie had to say to Jesse, she wanted no one else to hear.

She watched as he pushed his hands into his slacks' pockets, watching her carefully, his green eyes quiet, reflective, as she sat on the bed, dressed only in the short silk gown she had donned.

"Why do I have a feeling you want to talk first?" he quipped almost too seriously.

"Because you know me that well," she said softly, watching him a bit sadly. "You always have. Even when I was too young to know what it meant. And when I was too stupid to accept what it was."

He leaned against her dresser, watching her quietly. Terrie felt her chest tighten at the flood of emotion that washed over her. He was so strong, even now, as he watched her uncertainly, his eyes brilliant with all the emotions she had never realized were there before.

"You were never stupid, Terrie," he said quietly. "Frightened. Innocent..."

"And too stupid to know what I was feeling or what I wanted," she finished for him. "I love you, Jesse. I always have loved you."

He frowned, his expression brooding, intense. "I know that, Terrie. I always knew that."

She tilted her head. He wasn't lying. She could see just how very serious he was.

"And you love me," she whispered, fighting her tears. "You loved me, before Thomas."

He breathed out roughly. "Before Thomas, during Thomas, now," he growled. "Love doesn't just turn off, Terrie. What do you want me to say?"

It was there in his voice. Husky, controlled, endearingly honest. If there was one thing she knew about Jesse, it was that he would never lie to her about his feelings for her. He might not tell her something she needed to know, but he wouldn't lie to her.

"Why didn't you tell me?" she asked him roughly. "Why didn't you let me know, Jesse, instead of leaving me in the dark?"

"How, baby?" He shrugged, though she saw his fists clench in his pockets. "You were so scared of me you ran damned near every time I tried to get close. You've been like that ever since you realized I did want you. You ran, because who I was, what I was, frightened you."

It wasn't him. She stared at him in surprise. It had never been his needs that had her running.

She shook her head slowly. "I ran because my own feelings, my own needs, terrified me. Not you," she whispered. "You never frightened me, Jesse. Ever. But I scared the hell out of myself."

"Because of who I am. Because of what I wanted," he said roughly.

"Because of who I am." She shook her head quickly. "Don't you see, Jesse? It wasn't you. It was me. I couldn't make sense of my own needs, my own desires. I couldn't understand what I wanted."

"And now?" He looked so alone, so braced for her rejection.

She rose slowly to her feet, revealing the items she had left on the bed behind her. Handcuffs and leather ankle cuffs attached to chains. She saw his gaze flicker to them.

"Will you trust me to love you, Jesse?" she asked him softly. "I trust you. With everything I am. Everything you need. Will you trust me as well?"

Silence built within the room for long, intense seconds as he stared at the bed.

"I take it those aren't for you?" He nodded to the items.

She looked up at him from the corners of her eyes, a small smile playing at her lips. "No, they aren't for me."

He tensed, his expression darkening with such latent sensuality she felt her pussy creaming in response.

He cleared his throat. "No means no, Terrie," he reminded her firmly. "I can be man enough to give you want you want, within reason."

She smiled gently. "You've always given me more than I deserve, Jesse. But now, I want to give to you. My gift to you, because I love you."

He pulled his hands from his slacks, his fingers working slowly at the buttons of his shirt. He looked around the bedroom curiously.

"Why am I suddenly nervous?" he asked her with a half smile. A half-hearted attempt to remind her how dearly he loved being in control.

She moved to him, her hand lifting to touch his chest, reveling in the feel of the hard, warm muscle beneath his dark skin. She felt his breath quicken as she laid a kiss between the edges of his shirt as it fell open. His hands lifted, running up her back as he drew her closer.

"God, Terrie, you make me lose all my control. You know that?" He lowered his head, his lips pressing to her temple, her cheek, then her lips.

Terrie moaned in rising hunger as his tongue swept over her lips, licking at them, tasting her, savoring her as his arms tightened around her.

"That's only fair, because you do the same to me," she panted breathlessly against his tongue, then moaned in pleasure as his lips took control of hers, his tongue forging into her mouth in a stroke of heated pleasure.

His fingers clenched on the material of her gown. His body tightened. The small signs of his arousal, his need for her, built her own need higher. She moved against him, reveling in his kiss. His lips were hard, rough, yet incredibly gentle on hers. His tongue thrust into her mouth with forceful strokes, making her hungry for more and more of his taste.

His hands moved to her bare shoulders, smoothing over the flesh, making her tremble from the hot pleasure that streaked through her body. A touch so simple, she thought in awe, just his fingertips, yet her vagina clenched with the sharp darts of lightning-hot sensations they created.

His lips moved over hers slow and easy. So gentle. His very gentleness was at odds with the tension that made his body tighten, made him harder, stronger than ever before. The tenderness never changed. He groaned with rough hunger. His tongue plundered her mouth, mating erotically with hers, yet each touch was so controlled, so light and adoring it made her soul weep with the need it transmitted to her.

"Wait. Wait." She pulled back, aware that once again Jesse was giving. Overloading her senses, capturing her with a pleasure so seductively erotic she could do nothing but respond.

She couldn't lose control of herself, she thought frantically. This was for Jesse. His pleasure. His need. She had to return to him the bone tightening ecstasy he gave her each time he touched her.

"Terrie." He was panting for breath as he laid his forehead against hers, his hands, palms only, smoothing across her shoulders. "I need you so bad I'm shaking with it, baby. I could devour you now, standing here against this fucking wall."

"No." She shook her head, moving back from him until his hands caught at her hips, holding her still. "Please, Jesse." She stared up at him, knowing he wanted to give to her. Needed to give to her. But first, she needed to give to Jesse. "Let me do this, Jesse. Please. Just this once."

He groaned roughly, his head falling back against the wall as he stared up at the ceiling. "Terrie, you torture me all night and I promise I'll paddle your ass for sure."

"Promises, promises," she grinned as her fingers went to his belt. "Come on, Jesse, be brave."

He looked down at her as he toed his shoes from his feet, his abdomen clenching as her fingers stroked across it. "No piercings." He frowned fiercely. "You put a ring in my nipple, Terrie, and all bets are off. I'll have to retaliate."

She ran her fingers over the hard little pebble of his male nipple and grinned teasingly. "Gold would look good on you, Jesse. You should think about it."

He snorted roughly. "I don't think so, baby," he groaned as she slid the zipper of his slacks down, the backs of her fingers caressing the hard ridge of his cock beneath his silk boxers.

She removed the pants and boxers slowly, planting kisses down his hard thighs as she went. The muscles there tensed, his cock jerking as her tongue stroked his skin languidly.

"Son of a bitch, you're killing me," he groaned, his hands spearing through her hair as she blew a soft breath across his tightening scrotum.

"I'm loving you, Jesse. Loving you with everything I can give you." She leaned closer, her tongue stroking over the tightening sac. His legs spread for her, his cock so hard, the flesh stretched so tightly on it that it glistened in the candlelight.

His scrotum was bare of hair. She loved it. The sac was so silky, so soft with nothing to hinder her light strokes. His hands tightened in her hair as her teeth raked him gently, his hips pushing the flesh closer to her teasing tongue.

"God, Terrie." His voice was deep, strangled. "Your tongue is killing me, baby."

One last loving lick then she moved back, licking her lips as she rose from her kneeling position on the floor.

"On the bed," she whispered.

His gaze flickered to the cuffs. "Fuck," he breathed out roughly.

"We'll get there," she laughed softly. "In ways that will leave you screaming in pleasure."

"That screaming part." He glanced at her nervously. "Nothing too heavy, right?"

She lifted a brow. "Don't worry, Jesse, I promise not to breech any restricted areas."

He breathed out in relief. "I knew I loved you for a reason," he quipped. "Okay." He squared his shoulders with such a show of courage she had to smother her laughter. "Let's do this before I chicken out."

He plopped down on the bed, spreading his arms and legs with such reluctance she almost laughed out loud. Instead, she moved quickly to his wrists. She restrained them in the metal cuffs then clipped the other end to the chains that ran from the bottom of the bed rail. The leather cuffs were harder to attach, but within minutes she had his ankles restrained as well.

He watched her with narrowed eyes, the brilliant green heating to an almost dangerous level as she trailed her fingers up the inside of his taut leg. She took a deep breath. Despite Tally's plan, she had no intention of blindfolding him.

"Do you remember when I threatened to share you with one of my friends?" she asked him softly as she rose to her knees and pulled the silk gown quickly from her body.

His eyes widened. At first in surprise, then in growing heat. "What have you done, Terrie?"

"I want to give you a taste of what I know you'll give me eventually," she whispered. "Pleasure, Jesse. The most erotic pleasure I can think of for you. Would you let me do that? I can't do it without your permission."

His breathing was hard, rough. "Fuck. Tally." The moan wasn't one of pleasured anticipation. "I know damned well you wouldn't let anyone else in this room with us."

She could hear his nervousness now. "Terrie, honey, I would do anything in this world for you, you know that. But that woman is dangerous."

She moved from the bed, controlling her grin. "You didn't say no, Jesse," she reminded him. "Are you saying no?"

He cleared his throat. "No piercings, right?" His voice was thicker, almost slurred with his arousal.

"No piercings, Jesse," she promised as she turned on the light, held it a second, then turned it off again. "Should I blindfold you?"

"God, no!" he growled. "I'm going to watch, Terrie, every move you make. And baby, when your turn comes, I'm going to make you scream for mercy just as hard and as loud as you make me scream. You better remember that."

"I'm looking forward to it," she murmured as Tally stepped into the room. "You have no idea, Jesse, how much I'm looking forward to it."

Chapter Eleven

ꙮ

Jesse watched the two women carefully. He'd had a feeling, years ago, that Terrie could more than match his desires, but he'd be damned if he ever expected this.

Tally. Hell, he had suspected she was a wildcat, but he couldn't profess any driving desire for her. He had to admit she was damned pretty, though. Just a few inches shorter than Terrie, her skin a dark contrast to Terrie's creamy flesh. Her long black hair rippled down her back, her dark eyes glinted with amused desire.

"You owe me, boss," she murmured as she moved along his side, her lips whispering along his ear as Terrie moved to the other. "Big time."

A whiplash of scalding lust seared his body as Terrie's lips feathered over his neck. The twin sensations were stronger, more powerful than he had expected. He tugged at the restraints, his fingers curling into fists with his need to touch now. Two hands stroked over his chest, his abdomen, raising his blood pressure and his arousal level past heights he would have never dreamed it could.

Both hands were soft, silky and warm. Yet Terrie's held a heat, a gentleness he would have known anywhere. She stroked him as though her pleasure came from the touch of his skin alone. Not that Tally didn't know how to use her hands. Damned if she didn't. And her nails. Every muscle in his body clenched when she used them across his nipple. Shit, that shouldn't feel so damned good.

"Terrie," he growled her name as his gaze darkened with the spiraling pleasure.

It felt as though lips, tongues and seductive fingers were everywhere. His nipples, his chest, his abdomen. A wash of silken heat as Terrie's lips feathered toward his, Tally's drifting to his chest.

"Do you feel good, Jesse?" Terrie breathed against his lips, her eyes dark in the candlelight and filled with emotion.

"Kiss me, Terrie," he growled. "Before I go insane for your taste."

She smiled. A slow tilt of her lips that had his cock jerking in response. It was an erotic, captivating smile and had him groaning in sensual frustration. She leaned over him, her breasts brushing against his arm, his chest. The gold nipple ring taunted him as he glanced down, glowing against the rosy peak as she raked it across his chest.

Her lips touched his, her tongue stroked. His body bucked as Tally's lips moved to his chest, her tongue lapping at his nipple. Dammit, that wasn't supposed to feel that good.

But Terrie's kiss fried his brain. He struggled against the cuffs, desperate to touch her. He needed to touch her, to run his hands over her body, to show her with his touch, with his kiss, what she meant to him.

There was no escaping the bonds. No escaping the hot ecstasy moving over his body. Terrie's lips were silken fire on his as his head raised to get closer to the teasing kiss. Yet she was always just a breath away, licking at him, taunting him with the need for more.

Silken hands were like brush strokes of flame on his body when she finally came to him. Her tongue slipped into his mouth, her broken moan whispering around him as she took what she needed from the kiss. Deep, hungry, her tongue thrusting past his lips, tangling with his, stretching his senses on a rack of exquisite lust.

He groaned at the loss of her touch when she pulled back, his eyes opening, his gaze darkening as her teeth nipped at his jaw, then began to move lower. The scent of heated female need was like an aphrodisiac to his senses. It drifted around him, tightening his body to a flash point of sensitivity that was nearly painful.

"Feel good?" she breathed at his ear as her body began to move lower.

"You're killing me," he gasped, feeling Tally's lips and tongue stroking his abdomen, her hot little hands smoothing over his thighs.

"I'm loving you," she denied. "All of you, Jesse. Just let me love you."

Her lips stroked down his chest, his abdomen. He groaned in mounting pleasure, his cock throbbing, jerking, as they drew slowly closer to the center of his thighs.

Terrie was like a sleek little cat moving around him, her tongue licking at his skin, her teeth scraping sensually at his flesh. His body arched as their lips moved to his thighs. Hot, blistering with sensual delight, lips and tongue tortured his flesh, coming close to his desperate erection then moving back.

He was certain they were determined to drive him mad. Then he felt soft lips moving up the inside of one thigh, a quick adventurous stroke of a tongue on the smooth flesh of his scrotum.

"Terrie." He fought to arch closer as Terrie's tongue joined the game, licking up the shaft of his cock, swirling around the bulbous head.

He could feel his release nearing. His scrotum tightened with it, his body becoming electrified. It was so damned close, he knew he was within seconds of coming from the sheer eroticism of the act alone.

He looked down along his body to see Terrie laying beside him, her breasts brushing his thigh as her mouth moved slowly, adoringly over his cock. The tight, heavily veined flesh glistened from her saliva, jerked from the heated lash of her tongue. Her eyes were closed, her enjoyment in his response clearly written in her expression.

Below her, stretched between his spread thighs, Tally was busy torturing, tormenting his tightened scrotum. She licked and suckled, her teeth scraping erotically, her tongue laving him with brilliant heat.

Control was a thing of the past. Jesse existed only in the pleasure, the overriding exquisite torment the two women practiced on his restrained body. He fought the chains, his body bucking, rough, guttural growls sounding from his chest as he fought for his release.

Then Terrie's mouth tightened on him, drawing him deeper into her mouth, suckling the head of his cock with a deep, rhythmic flexing of her mouth and tongue that proved to be too much when combined with Tally's mouthing of his scrotum below.

His hoarse shout was torn from his chest as he felt his release explode through his body. His head arched back, grinding into the mattress beneath him as his hips arched higher to Terrie's tormenting suckling. Destructive quakes of sensation ripped through his body, his testicles, shooting his semen from the tip of his cock as though it were the first release of his life.

"Terrie. Son of a bitch!" His cry was torn from his very soul as the pleasure rocked him, shuddered through him, left him gasping in an aftermath so intense he wondered if he would ever truly recover.

Chapter Twelve

ꟸ

Terrie dragged herself slowly out of bed the next morning. Her body ached pleasantly, drawing a satisfied smile to her lips. Jesse had been uncontrollable after the cuffs had come off. God only knew when Tally finally left, because from the minute he gained his freedom Jesse had flipped Terrie on her back, his cock thrusting hard and fast inside her, and he hadn't stopped for hours.

Dawn had been peeking through the bedroom when he collapsed beside her, swearing she was going to pay for that loss of control. Moving into the shower she stood beneath the steamy water, her eyes closed, reveling in the memory of Jesse's hoarse shouts of release, his steamy, sexy words as he praised her body, her sexuality. It had been the most amazing night of her life.

Leaning against the shower wall she soaped her bath sponge, her heart pounding in a hard rhythm as nerves began to take hold of her once again. She knew what was coming and though it didn't frighten her, she wondered at the changes in herself. Jesse had always been so much a part of her life. For years he had been there, and though she had tried not to lean on him she had known he was there if the need arose.

Always there. She bit her lip as the thought crossed her mind. Always waiting, always wanting, just as she had. Always wanting the one thing, the one part of herself that frightened her more than anything else did.

Was she brave enough to be the woman Jesse needed? She moved the sponge slowly over her breasts, shivering at the sensitivity of her own body. Yeah, she thought with another smile, she could do it. Surely she could.

She wasn't nearly finished with Jesse Wyman either. He had whispered the words she needed to hear as sleep overtook her that morning, but he had yet to say them to her while she was fully awake. Terrie wanted to see him, to know he meant it when he shared his love with her. He had said the words hesitantly, as though uncertain of her reaction or her awareness.

I've always loved you. His voice had been incredibly soft, the rough timber hoarse, thick with emotion, unlike anything she had heard from Jesse before. As she dressed, she vowed that once and for all, before this relationship went any further, she and Jesse had to talk. There was too much between them, too many secrets, too many words unspoken. It was time to clear it away. Time to accept the past, not just for her, but for Jesse as well.

Thomas had left an inheritance of pain and bitter regret with many of his actions and his brutal cruelty. Somehow he had known that Jesse cared about her, just as he had guessed her feelings for Jesse. He had used those emotions and deceived both of them in his drive to hurt as many people as he could. As though only in stripping them bare, in seeing the agony he created, could he find any happiness in his life.

Terrie shook her head at the thought of that. She needed answers herself. She needed to know once and for all where she and Jesse were headed. She quickly dried her body, moving into the bedroom to dress before heading to Jesse's office.

As she entered the room the phone rang demandingly.

"Yes?" She grabbed the receiver as she began to search her dresser drawer for just the right undergarments.

"How about lunch?" His dark voice had her shivering, her cunt pulsing with demanding need as she closed her eyes to savor the sound.

"Where?" Her voice was husky. She refused to attempt to hide her need now. He knew her, knew she could no longer resist the pleasure he could give her.

"My office, whenever you show up," he said softly. "I have to take care of a few things first, then I'll be free the rest of the day."

The rest of the day to play. She fought to keep from panting like an inexperienced teenager at the thought of it. She managed it, but only barely.

"Sounds good." She pulled a midnight blue thong from her dresser and a matching silk push-up bra as she fought to try to breathe properly.

"Terrie." His voice was smooth, low, a sexual stroke of pleasure across her senses.

She swallowed tightly. "Yes, Jesse?"

"Use the butt plug again, and that pretty little violet slip dress hanging in your closet. And no bra, Terrie."

The dominant, ruthless sound of his voice had her trembling in nervous anticipation.

"Maybe..."

"Terrie." There was an edge to his voice now that had her pussy quaking in reaction. "Be wearing it or I promise you, you'll wish you had."

The line disconnected.

Terrie stared down at the receiver for a shocked second before she laughed softly. Oh, now there was a man fighting for control. Desperately. He was a dominant alpha male scrambling to reassert his authority. She loved it. She wondered how quickly she could throw him off balance once again? Drawing in a deep breath, smiling in anticipation, she vowed to find out.

* * * * *

"Men are so predictable." Tally closed the door behind her as Jesse hung up the phone and drew in a deep, hard breath.

He arched a brow sarcastically. "Did I ring you, Tally?"

She rolled her eyes expressively. The woman was a menace. He had known she was a menace when he hired her the year before; he was even more convinced of it now.

"You know Jesse, we've known each other a long time." She sat down regally in the chair across from him, smoothing out her skirt rather absently before glancing up at him again. Cool as a cucumber, that was Tally.

"We have," he admitted carefully, wondering where she was going with this.

"I've known Terrie even longer," she sighed patiently. "She's such a brave little thing when she wants to be. But that bravery is not going to extend to a scheduled ménage, such as you and your buddies like to set up. If you want her, you're going to have to surprise her. Dare her." Tally's voice was a dare itself. "But once she does it, I'm certain she'll settle right into your little domination games."

She leaned back in her chair, her attitude one of mocking acceptance of an eccentricity she found little amusement in.

"You know, Tally." He leaned forward in his chair, controlling his grin. "As you stated, we've known each other for quite a while. And don't think you're the only one of us who can read easily between the lines."

Her eyes widened in false surprise. "Sweetie, I never imagined such a thing." She shook her head tolerantly. "You do get the strangest ideas."

"Tally, I'm not nearly as simple as you are giving me credit for," he warned her carefully, allowing her to see the core of steady purpose he kept carefully below the surface. "I know many of your little secrets, sweetheart, and don't think for a minute you'll get away with baiting the group forever."

"Oh them." She waved her hand carelessly. "I'd worry less about your playmates and more about your lover if I were you." She grinned. "Terrie will keep stealing your control, Jesse, if you don't do something quickly. She can be a dominant little thing, can't she?" She chuckled wickedly.

Jesse remained quiet, calm, though his amusement was growing. Tally was supremely confident, mocking, more than a little dominant herself. He couldn't wait to see her fall.

"Tally, you have the rest of the day off," he told her softly. "Long lunch, early dinner. I'll see you tomorrow."

She sighed, and he was intrigued to see the impression of a pout forming along her lips before she carefully controlled it.

"So who is the playmate going to be?" She tried to come off as casual, curious, but he caught the hint of something more.

He leaned closer to his desk, tilting his head with amused inquiry. "Who would you suggest, Tally?"

She shrugged negligently. "I was merely curious, Jesse."

"Is there someone who shouldn't be considered, Tally?" He leaned back in his chair, watching her carefully.

She came gracefully to her feet. "You and your little playmates are really none of my concern. By the way, Lucian Conover called. He's coming in after lunch to discuss something about that contract he had problems with," she sniffed disdainfully. "He didn't want to hear that you might be busy. I'll go to lunch now, dear. Watch out for hidden handcuffs and the like." Her amused laughter was soft, lilting in its confidence.

"Tally." He stopped her as she neared the door.

"Yes, Jesse." She turned back, her body poised gracefully to sweep from the room.

"Lucian likes handcuffs, sweetheart, and a whole lot more. You might want to watch how much you taunt him."

Her grin turned wicked, decidedly sexual. "Oh Jesse, darling, don't worry. I won't hurt him too badly."

He chuckled as she swept from the room. He knew Lucian would eventually make his move on the temperamental little beauty; he just wondered if the other man would survive it.

Chapter Thirteen

ꕥ

The outer office was deserted. Terrie drew in a deep breath, fighting the trembling ache in her rear from the plug inserted inside it. The silk of the dress rasped against her sensitive nipples. Her pussy creamed heatedly. To some extent she suspected what was coming. The added rush of nervous fear and anticipation had her nearly panting in arousal.

She turned the lock in the door as she closed it behind her. The main offices were quiet this afternoon but she wanted to take no chances that she and Jesse would be disturbed.

She had given to Jesse the night before in the only way she knew how, to show him she understood the needs and the desires that were so much a part of him. She even understood, to some extent, that need as well. Watching Tally touch him, seeing his arousal, his pleasure, hearing his breathing hitch as he let the pleasure suffuse him, had been incredibly arousing.

In setting up the experience she was more than aware she had given Jesse implicit permission to turn the tables on her. She had given him her acceptance without words and now she fought to stem her nervousness over the choice. She had never been taken in such a way. Had never been shared between two men. Until Jesse, she had never known such rough loving, that such incredible, spiraling pleasure could be attained from the darker edge of lust.

She bit her lip as she approached his door. It was barely open, with no sound coming from the room beyond. Somehow he had managed to find his control once again. She could sense it, knew it. His voice on the phone earlier had assured her of it.

She pushed the door open slowly, stepping into the room as her gaze sought out Jesse.

He stood in front of the large, drapery-shrouded windows. The room was dim; his form was tall, graceful, commanding.

"Lock the door." His voice was a hard rumble of lust.

Terrie felt her womb clench, her pussy flood. With shaking hands she closed the door, turning the lock and nearly flinching at the sharp sound it made. She stood silently, watching him, trying not to pant with her own rising sexual demands. She could feel her nipples hardening further, her cunt clenching in excruciating need.

Her eyes were drawn to the low table in front of the leather couch. Terrie drew in a deep breath to keep from whimpering. Lying on the table was a tube of lubrication, two small nipple clamps and a jelly dildo perhaps half the width of his cock, but just as long. Her gaze returned to him.

She started as he moved. A ripple of motion as he walked to the low table, glancing down at the articles then back to her.

"You've known me for a long time, Terrie," he said softly. "I've never made an effort to hide who I am or what I enjoy from you."

He paused for long moments as though waiting to see if she would deny his words. She couldn't. She had known all along.

"Others would call me perverted…depraved," he continued. "I won't deny that, either. It's definitely not conventional, but it's who I am. And it's a desire you can't deny in yourself, Terrie. Not any longer."

She wasn't attempting to deny it, but she would be damned if she knew now what to do. She licked her lips nervously, aware that his eyes narrowed on the movement.

"I haven't denied it, Jesse," she finally said softly.

A small smile quirked his lips. "No, you haven't." He lifted his arm, extending his hand out to her. "Come here, Terrie."

She walked to him slowly, trembling, achingly aware of her body and the sexual fire coursing through it. She felt as though flames were leaping in her cunt, burning clear to her soul. As she stepped close to him the heat seared her body, her breasts, her anus. She nearly shuddered from the hunger to feel him thrusting hard and heavy inside her. Dominating her. Giving the gift of her own surrender, her complete submission to her own needs.

His hands slid up her arms. Terrie drew in a hard breath, her hunger for him nearly overcoming any semblance of control she could have possessed. Her flesh prickled, small goose bumps rising at the calloused touch of his palms, the warmth of his body.

"Do you know how beautiful you are to me?" he asked her as his fingers moved to the small buttons of her dress, slipping the first one free. "How long I've waited to touch you, how many nights I laid in a fever of rage while Thomas lived? Praying to God he wouldn't touch you, wouldn't hurt you?"

She shook her head, fighting those memories.

"I'll have no more lies between us, Terrie. No more secrets." He leaned close, his lips feathering her ear as he whispered, "Do you know how hard it was to walk away the nights I came to dinner while he lived, his permission to fuck you ringing in my ears? My need to hear you scream my name pounding in my cock?"

Her eyes widened in shock at the near violence in his tone.

"I'm sorry." She trembled in his grip. "I didn't know. I was so frightened of…this." She shuddered as he nipped at her ear lobe.

"You're mine," he growled. "Your pleasure, your cries, your sweet pussy, your tight ass. It's mine, Terrie. All of it. To pleasure how I see fit. To tempt, to tease, to watch as you experience every sexual fantasy you could have ever dreamed."

Before she could have guessed his intentions, his hand hooked in the front of her dress and with a quick motion jerked the fabric apart. Buttons scattered as she gasped in surprise, only to moan in pleasure as his lips covered hers, his tongue sinking past her parted lips into the moist interior of her mouth.

He jerked the tattered remains of silk from her body a second before his arms crushed her to his chest. The Egyptian cotton of his shirt rasped her nipples, burning her with sensation as his lips moved on hers hungrily, his tongue thrusting between her lips, licking at hers, twining with it as she moaned in rising need.

Between her thighs her pussy spasmed, creaming furiously as the weight of the nipple ring tugged at the sensitive peak of one breast. One hand moved to the heavy weight of her hair as he pulled her head farther back, his lips moving down her neck, stroking tingling electric arcs of sensation over her flesh before he raised his head and stared down at her with dark arousal.

She stood panting, swaying as he moved back from her. Reaching down he picked up the two nipple clamps as she swallowed tightly. Her gaze met his as he watched her closely, the little jeweled clamps held in his hand.

His head lowered to her breasts.

"Jesse." Her whimper was part fear, part incredible need as his tongue began to lick, his lips to suckle until her nipples stood out hard and aching from the mounds of her breasts.

"Just a little hurt," he whispered. "But you like a little hurt, don't you, Terrie?"

He attached the first clamp; its firm, nipping pressure had her nearly climaxing from the pleasure/pain alone. She couldn't hold back her cry as he applied the mate to her other nipple. She was swaying, her pussy gushing its thick juice as the sensations threatened to overwhelm her.

His finger pushed at the little jewels dangling from the clamp and she bit her lip at the tug on her furiously aroused flesh.

"Jesse, I don't know if I can stand it." The pleasure and the pain were swamping her.

His fingers reached up to her cheek, touching her gently, lovingly. "When it's too much, Terrie, just say so. I won't take from you, baby. I want to give to you."

She bit her lip at the emotion in his voice. It throbbed with his need to show her all he was, echoed with his own deep, dark desires.

"Lie down on the couch. On your stomach." His voice was harsh with his fight for control. "Raise your hips. Let me see how well your ass is filled with that plug."

She nearly sank to the carpet with the burst of weakening lust that surged through her body. She did as he commanded, stretching out on the cool, fitted coverlet that stretched over the leather couch. She positioned her body as he had demanded, shivering at the thought of his gaze going to the base of the thick plug stretching her.

"Beautiful," he muttered, a second before she heard him undressing.

Agonized desire rushed through her body. The clamps on her nipples weren't overly tight; the pressure was killing her with her need for more. A second later more came.

There was no warning. Not a sound to indicate his intentions. His hand landed firmly, heatedly on one rounded cheek of her rear. Terrie cried out, but rather than pain, pleasure tore a destructive path through her body as her pussy raged in furious demand. A second later, another blow landed on the other cheek. She flinched, crying out, though her hips arched back for more.

She couldn't stand it. Searing lust swept through her, overtaking her in ways she would have never imagined.

Within minutes her ass was burning, her cunt dripping, weeping in greedy need.

"You have the most beautiful ass I have ever seen on a woman," he said as his hand then smoothed over the aching flesh. "Do you know how many nights I've jacked off thinking about fucking your sweet ass, Terrie?"

Chapter Fourteen

ꝏ

Terrie whimpered. Her muscles clenched around the plug that stretched her, anticipating the harder, hotter invasion of his thick cock inside her. Her buttocks were hot from the fiery sting of his hand, her cunt an inferno of unslaked arousal.

"Mine," he whispered again as his mouth feathered over the heated curve of one buttock, causing her to jerk at the pleasure ricocheting through her system. "But first, I want you ready for me."

He moved between her thighs, his hand at her hip, urging her to raise herself further. Terrie clenched her fists into the coverlet over the couch, bending her knees to raise herself to him. His hard, tight moan of approval had her juices spilling copiously from her hot pussy.

Terrie shuddered as she felt his fingers grip the base of the plug before moving it slowly from her body. The wide anchor stretched her heatedly, causing her to whimper in growing arousal then in loss as it slid completely from her. But Jesse had no intentions of leaving her wanting.

She heard him moving. Heard the cap on the tube of lubrication gel snap, then felt the thick application of it at her back entrance as his fingers pushed inside her briefly.

"I wanted to start easy," he whispered as his arm hooked around her waist to draw her back with him as he half reclined against the couch behind her. "First the dildo and me, then we'd advance, but I don't think I can wait, Terrie."

She struggled for a sense of balance as his hands moved her, bringing her over his hips, placing her legs on each side of him, her back to him as his cock nudged at her anal opening.

She shuddered, her hands gripping his wrists where they held her waist, her rear entrance fluttering open as he pressed his cock into it.

"Oh God, Jesse!" She could feel the thick flesh of her anus opening to the flared head of his cock as he pressed her closer.

Heat shot through her pussy, her rectum and up her spine as she felt her muscles part slowly for him. The hard bite of pain, the fiery wash of arousal, all combining to push her past her preconceived notions of lust. The need was like a demon inside her, fighting to be free as Jesse slowly slid into the well-greased channel.

She chanted his name as she felt each inch slip into her ass. Deliberately, slowly.

"Terrie, you're so tight," he whispered as the bulging head finally pressed home. "So hot and sweet, baby."

She screamed. She couldn't help it. His cock slid to the hilt inside her in one smooth stroke, forging into her hot ass as pleasure/pain whipped violently through her body. She could feel the juices dripping from her cunt, her clamped nipples throbbing in response as he drew her back against his chest.

"Easy, baby." He pressed kisses to her shoulder, his tongue stroking her flesh. "Just a minute, baby. Just get used to it. It's okay."

She was gasping, but not just in pain, though the pressure was biting. In pleasure. In an agony of need. She could feel her orgasm building in her very womb.

"Jesse, help me," she whispered desperately, the fingers of one hand going to her pussy, circling her swollen clit as she undulated against him.

Oh God. That was good. She moved again, one foot slipping to the floor to anchor her as her body arched in reflex, driving his cock deeper inside her as she changed position.

She was sobbing with the pleasure now, her fingers moving frantically to the entrance of her aching pussy only to have Jesse catch them, hold them back as his hips flexed, pulling his cock back mere inches and then driving it forward again.

She writhed on the impalement, fighting to free her hands as harsh cries fell from her lips. She was so hot, so aroused she felt as though she would burst into flames at any minute.

"Jesse, I can't take this," she cried out as one of his hands held hers while the other helped lift her hips enough to allow him to begin a series of those easy thrusts into her ass.

She was breaking apart. She could feel her cunt tightening, spasming, begging to be filled. She was within seconds of screaming out that need when the lock to the office door clicked and the door slowly opened.

Lucian Conover stepped into the room, pocketing the key as he moved to the couch. His fingers began working quickly at the buttons of his shirt.

"Terrie?" Jesse whispered her name as his cock throbbed inside her tight ass.

She stared up at Lucian, knowing her cunt caught his gaze, the glistening juices that covered the bare folds as Jesse raided her anus. He undressed quickly, his cock springing free as he dropped his pants, the thickly veined shaft engorged and more than ready to fill her.

"Is this what you want, Terrie?" Lucian asked her as one hand went to his thick erection. "I'll leave if you want me to."

But did she want him to? Her eyes strayed to his cock as her mind filled with the erotic thoughts of him filling her, easing the blistering need that tormented her pussy.

He bent to his knees, spreading her legs further, his head lowering to her swollen clit as Jesse began to thrust slowly in and out of her ass once again. Their half reclining position allowed him to pull his cock free by several inches before powering it home again, rocking her body with the streaking pleasure/pain as Lucian's suckling mouth locked onto her clit. It didn't take long before the beginnings of the first explosive orgasm ripped through Terrie's body. She tightened, crying out, fighting for balance when Jesse lifted his hands, gripped the nipple clamps and released her tormented flesh as the first explosion tore through her.

She had no more than screamed his name when Lucian came to his feet, bending his knees and began to work his cock into the convulsing muscles of her pussy.

"Easy, baby. There, sweetheart. Feel how good it can be. Feel, Terrie, just how fucking good it can be." He stilled beneath her as Lucian began to fuck inside her with slow, short strokes, pushing his bulging cock deeper inside the fist-tight confines of her pussy.

Her eyes widened, her gaze darkening as Jesse continued to croon at her ear, his cock throbbing in her ass as Lucian worked his impressive erection deep inside the tightened channel of her cunt.

She was gasping, begging, distantly amazed that the cries and pleas were coming from her own throat.

"Yes." Her head fell back on Jesse's shoulder as his lips pressed to her cheek. "Yes. God. Fuck me. Jesse, make him fuck me hard, before I die."

Her hoarse words acted as a catalyst on the two men. She didn't know whose hands supported her above Jesse's body; she didn't care. In perfect synchronization she felt Jesse's cock slide nearly free of the grip of her ass while Lucian's thrusted, strong and sure, deep into her gripping pussy. Lucian pulled back, only to have Jesse surge inside the clasping heat of her ass.

The dual penetrations were more than her heightened emotions and overly sensitive body could process at once. As they began to fuck her hard and fast, their groans blending with her feminine cries, she tumbled headlong into an orgasm so explosive, so violent she lost her breath, lost her control and surrendered herself to the cyclonic whiplash of emotion and pleasure/pain that ripped through her body. Lucian and Jesse groaned her name and began spurting their own releases deep inside her spasming channels.

Chapter Fifteen

ஐ

"There, baby..." It wasn't over. Hours later Terrie trembled, her body soaked with perspiration as yet another orgasm tore through her.

Jesse's cock was spurting heavily up into her swollen pussy, as Lucian once again gained his release in the tight recess of her ass. There had been little respite in the hours they had pleasured her. Jesse had held her once, watching, whispering explicit directions to her as they both watched Lucian part the lips of her cunt, his cock stroking slowly inside her, driving her insane as Jesse told her how beautiful it was, whispered to her how beautiful she was in her pleasure.

And the pleasure was never ending.

There was little resistance in her when they finally pulled free of her body and Jesse helped her collapse weakly to the couch. Night had fallen, the offices she knew were empty and she was too replete, too satisfied to even consider moving now.

She felt the soft sheet drape her body as her eyes closed in weariness, only dimly aware of Jesse and Lucian dressing.

* * * * *

Jesse watched her. Weariness dragging at his limbs as he zipped his slacks and watched Lucian re-button his own shirt. The other man was quiet, reflective, as he glanced at Terrie. Her hair flowed over her shoulders, clinging damply to the moist flesh as she drifted into sleep.

"Thomas didn't deserve her," Lucian sighed as her breathing deepened.

"I do, Lucian." Jesse was very well aware of the fact that there were several of the members of their group who had had their eye on Terrie even before Thomas's death. "She's mine."

Lucian nodded sharply. He more than the others, Jesse knew, had been interested. Just as he knew that any woman who accepted Conover would likely be biting off more than she could chew.

"She's a one-man woman," Lucian sighed, grinning rakishly. "I doubt she would appreciate the plans I had for her."

"Wrong woman," Jesse agreed.

Lucian nodded again. "Take care of her, Jesse. She loves you, you know."

Yeah, he knew that, Jesse thought. She had proved that the night before in ways he would have never imagined.

"As I love her, Lucian," he sighed. He always had. For as long as he had known her.

Lucian nodded abruptly then left the office with a quick, purposeful stride. Jesse shook his head as he collapsed in the chair across from Terrie and watched her sleep.

She was the most beautiful thing in the world to him. For years he had feared he would have to eventually restrain his sexuality to have her. Tamp down the need to see her surrendering to the ultimate pleasure. That of allowing her body to be completely, overwhelmingly submissive to her own desires. To take the greatest gift he had to offer her. The gift of her complete, uninhibited sexuality.

Some women had that hidden core, the darker desires, the search for the ultimate pleasure. Just as Jesse and those like him held the male half of that core. The need to see and to feel the surrender of their women to that hidden sexuality. To watch someone they trusted, someone they knew, tapping into the dark desires and sensuality of their women. It was an ultimate high, a release unlike any other.

Not that it would happen often. But sometimes. Sighing, he moved to the office closet and removed the dress he had brought for her that evening. He laid it across the chair as he moved to her once again.

"Wake up, baby," he whispered as he lifted her into his arms and headed for the shower on the other side of his office. "Come on. Time to plan the rest of our lives."

She opened her eyes, drowsy, seductive and her lips quirking into a temptress's smile.

"Rest of our lives, huh?" She looped her arms lazily around his shoulders, staring up at him, loving him. He could feel her love, the warmth that spread over him when he watched her.

"The rest of our lives." He put her down in the bathroom, staring down at her. "I love you, Terrie. You have to know that by now."

Her smile lit up his soul. "I love you, Jesse. But this sharing thing." She rubbed hesitantly at her ear. "Let's keep this to a minimum," she suggested softly. "I really prefer you."

He chuckled, wrapping his arms around her, wishing he had the energy to throw her to the floor and fuck her again. Just for the sheer pleasure of it.

"Definitely a minimum," he promised as he drew back from her, staring down at her, adoring her. "Just when you need it, baby. I promise, just when you need it."

Epilogue

ꙮ

"Hi Jaded, how's tricks?" The words popped up on the computer screen, drawing an amused smile to Tally's lips.

"Slow, Wicked. Very slow," she typed back, snorting at the understatement.

The online life she led was the complete opposite of the real life she escaped each evening that she had the chance. The same men, the same parties, the same crap. She had grown bored with the endless round months ago. Why she had grown bored she had yet to figure out.

"Your boss still doing his own files?" It was a running joke in the online chat rooms she inhabited. She had told the story the first day it had occurred. Everyone had seemed awed by her accomplishment. She had personally hoped for at least a good argument out of Jesse Wyman at the time. She hadn't expected him to actually do his own fucking files.

"Hell if I know," she finally typed in. *"I think he fired me today."*

Repositioning, firing, it was the same thing. She liked working with Wyman. It wasn't exactly challenging but it left her plenty of time for shopping.

"Fired?" The words popped back. *"He wouldn't dare fire you."*

She laughed to herself. There were days Wyman had wanted to kill her, but he had resisted the urge with more self-control than she had given him credit for. Of course, the wedding Terrie was planning was keeping him pretty tired. That or her afternoon visits to his office.

"He says it's repositioning. He sent me to hell, Wicked." She sighed at the thought.

The merger between Conover's and Delacourte's had been more than a surprise last month. Even bigger was the surprise that she would now be the personal assistant for Lucian Conover.

"Repositioning?" The short question was so typical of Wicked. She could almost feel his impatience. *"In Hell?"*

"In Hell." She sighed. *"My new boss is Lucifer. This is not going to be fun. There goes all my playtime. (pout)"* She typed in the expression even as she did so huffily. Lucian Conover was not her idea of the perfect boss. *"Let's hope he's at least hiding a sense of humor under that scowl he wears. I bet he doesn't even know the difference between a ménage and margarita. Who will I tell all my dirty jokes to?"*

* * * * *

Lucian scowled. Son of a bitch. Lucifer, was he? Didn't know a ménage from a margarita? He bit off a series of volatile curses as he jumped up from the computer and paced the den furiously. Smart-mouthed, viperous little termagant. He could show her a fucking ménage she would still remember into her next life if she kept this shit up. She had no sense of decorum and had shown him zero respect each time he showed up at Jesse's office.

She stung him with that viperous tongue of hers, smirked every chance she had and showed in a hundred different ways that she expected him to grovel at the perfection of her tiny feet. Son of a bitch. For a taste of that sweet little body he just might do it, too, and that was what really rankled.

"You still breathing?" Her tart question came over the instant message with a soft ring.

"Yeah, just wondering what the connection was between the ménage and the margarita," he typed in, damning himself a

thousand different ways. He was insane to have demanded her as his personal assistant. He had lost his ever lovin' mind.

"No connection." He paused at her answer, frowning. Jaded always had a reason for damned near everything she said. Unless she was unhappy. Unless she was lonely. He had learned that over the past year. Had made it his business to learn everything he could about her.

"You okay, Jaded?" He really shouldn't care, but he did.

"Oh yes, I'm fine." Her words rang hollow, even through the impersonal communication box. *"Maybe I'll go shopping tomorrow. I hear there's a sale on shoes…"*

"Uh oh. Poor cows, sacrificing their lives to support your addiction." He shook his head, yet still he worried. She wasn't acting normal.

"Cows, alligators, whatever." Nope, that wasn't his Jaded.

"Hey babe, you can talk to me, you know." He needed her to.

There was a long silence.

"She's my friend." The words finally came through with a sense of sadness. *"I can't believe she has such horrid taste in men."*

"Yeah?" He didn't even pretend to understand that one.

"I love her like a sister." She had to be talking about Terrie.

He waited to see what else she said.

"I can't believe she actually fucked Lucifer! Was she insane? Has she lost her mind? The man is an outcast. He has no style. No class, and I doubt he has a cock over five inches long. He probably only needs a finger or two to jack off with."

He sat back slowly in his chair. His cock, all five inches and several more, pulsed in outrage. His eyes narrowed.

"The man scowls. He sneers. Stomps around like a bull in a china shop. He is such a bore. Geez. I need a new job."

His fists clenched, his teeth ground together as he saw red. The viperous little witch. A bull in a china shop? Five-inch cock? Five-inch cock?? Ohh, he would show her a hell of a lot fucking more than five inches. Damn her. The woman had a bite that would do a rabid dog proud.

"If you quit, just think of all the shoes that would cry." *It was lame. Real lame, but he'd be damned if he could type his outrage to her over the Internet. She would probably save the fucking message to show all her chat room buddies. He sneered. Oh, was she in for a surprise.*

"Well, this is true. But I'm definitely looking."

He stilled. Looking, was she? He'd see about that one.

"Well, good luck darlin'. Now I'm off. Hot date tonight."

Nothing came back for long moments.

"All right. Goodnight."

"Night, darlin'. Cheer up, maybe you'll get lucky and he'll at least have more than five inches." *He growled.*

"As though that can help him." *He could almost hear the haughty vibration of the words.* "Where oh where have all the alphas gone? Your mothers must have breast-fed you overly long."

"Or yours fed you venom and spice rather than sweet milk," *he typed back furiously. And he meant it.*

"LOL. Good one, Wicked. Have fun for me while you're out. Talk to you later."

He clicked the box away. He shut down the program, damn near shaking with rage and arousal. He came to his feet, pushing his fingers ruthlessly through his hair as he clenched his teeth against his anger. Damn her. Lucifer, was he? Five inches, was he? He snarled as he stomped through the house, jerking the leather jacket from the staircase post as he headed for the door.

Miss Jaded Tally was in for one hell of a surprise.

Enjoy an excerpt from:
MÉNAGE A MAGICK

Chapter One

ꝏ

The soft glow from the aura of magick that surrounded the twin moons of Sentmar was slowly dissipating. The twin rings were thinner than they had been in the entire written history of the planet. Once, thick luminous rings surrounded the moons, like pillowy circles of thick, rich cream. They were now wispy, and more transparent than ever before.

The magick of the land was growing weaker by the year now, instead of by the decade. They would have to move quickly, or it would be too late. The humans would once again rule the land and they would have no mercy for their magick counterparts.

Lasan stood on the upper balcony of the Veraga castle and stared into the night sky, frowning as he observed the phenomena. All that was Sentmar and magick was now threatened. All that had balanced justice and peace within their world was at stake.

"We must move quickly." Drago, his twin, stood behind him, staring at the moons as well, his voice soft, concerned. "She will not see reason, Lasan. Not until after the Joining. We can no longer afford to hesitate."

He was growing impatient. Lasan could feel it beating at his brain, his twin's impatience. It saddened him, concerned him. Drago, for all his stubborn disposition and determination, was rarely impatient. Lasan's natural patience had always served to stem the stubborn streak that ran through his brother.

He pushed his fingers wearily through his hair, then clasped the balustrade with an iron grip.

"We will contact Queen Amoria on the morrow," he decided. "As you say, we can wait no longer."

Queen Amoria, ruler of the house of Sellane, the ruling family of the Covenani, the sect of sorceresses that had separated themselves hundreds of years ago from the Wizards destined to complete them. Without her aid, they would be unable to approach the Princess Brianna in any manner.

Lasan had never completely understood the separation. Time had hidden the answers to his questions, and the Wizard Sentinels were silent when he came to them with his need for answers. All he and Drago knew was that they were to fix the separation. It was now their destiny, the responsibility of their world rested on their shoulders alone.

To preserve all they held dear, the woman they would have wooed to their hearts would have to be forced to their bed. It was a bitter thought to swallow. The one woman created to complete them, to bind them forever within a ring of magick, pleasure and satisfaction, had denied them.

Contemptuously, sneeringly, she had thrown their offer of Joining back in their faces, denying any link they could have shared. She was their natural Consort, and yet she ran from them at every chance.

But wasn't that what the Covenani were good at, Drago snapped within his mind. *They ran from our ancestors as this one now runs from us. Mocking the bonds between us, and her own needs.*

And this was so. They could feel the arousal that pulsed in her body when last they had touched her. Holding her between them, the heat of her body, the magick rising inside her, tormenting them with a level of lust they had never known before.

As Lasan had caressed her soft lips, Drago had smoothed his lips over her satin shoulders, exploring the softness of her flesh, warming her between them, allowing her to feel the pleasure that rose from each touch.

She had shivered in their arms, whimpered as her mouth opened, accepting a deeper kiss, a firmer caress. They had been inflamed by her response, the magick soaring through their bodies, rising, building to an aura that would have encompassed them all, forging the bond to come.

It had been then that Brianna had broken away from them. Gasping for air, shock rounding her violet eyes, her own power glittering in the dark orbs as she faced them furiously.

"Dwell on this no longer," Drago bit out from behind him. "She will come to us, Lasan. We will give her no other choice."

Lasan sighed deeply. "But perhaps it is a choice she needs to make," he murmured. "For all our future happiness."

"It is the Joining that is required, not her happiness," his brother growled.

Lasan was well aware that Drago regretted this as much as he did. They had given her every opportunity to make the choice for herself. They had all but gone to their knees in supplication. It rankled at their pride.

"Begin preparations," Lasan sighed.

They would need several sets of Wizard Twins to accompany them, as well as the Sentinel Guards, the magickal warriors who kept a tight rein on the darkness that would have invaded their lands.

"She is ours, Lasan," Drago growled. "I do not completely understand your hesitancy in this. She will come to accept us."

Lasan turned and stared at his brother. The night breeze whipped the long black hair back from his face, revealing the strong, determined lines of his expression. His eyes were a dark, emerald green, piercing and brilliant. His cheekbones high, his jaw squared and tight with his anger.

Lasan shook his head. Self-mockery filled him. He knew well that Drago's anger stemmed from his own reluctance to force this alliance. His anger that she had denied them, despite her needs, despite the knowledge that filled her, that she did indeed desire them.

Despite their powers, the advanced degree of magick that filled them, they could not break through her reserve, they could not ease whatever fears filled her enough to allow her to accept them.

"The Seculars are gaining in strength, and the dark force propelling them is gaining ground. We cannot afford even the time we have allowed her thus far," Drago reminded him. "I have called the Sashtain Twins, as well as the Alessi. They must begin to press their suits quickly if this is to succeed."

Lasan nodded firmly. "We will begin preparations to leave then. The Covenani Ball begins in two moon cycles. Ensure a fair number of Twin sets are in attendance. Cauldaran and Covenani can be separated no longer."

A millennia apart, and still the female sect of magick keepers had not returned to their male counterparts, nor expressed a desire in reaching concessions. Queen Amoria would have to see the dangers in this, whether she wanted to or not.

He knew the woman to be a good ruler, a woman said to have her people's welfare at heart. As a Queen, she was more respected than any of her predecessors. But she was still a Sorceress, and possibly determined to continue the separation out of pride and fear of the unknown.

Lasan cursed silently as he turned and stared back at the brilliant glow of the moons. The peace that the land had enjoyed for so many thousands of years could now come to an end if they did not move quickly. He closed his eyes, thinking of Brianna, her warmth, her passion. He sent his touch out to her, a most difficult maneuver considering the distance that separated them. He felt Drago's power join with his, despite the other duties he carried out.

A smile tipped Lasan's lips as he felt her sleepy response, heard her moan of passion. *Enjoy,* he whispered silently. *We come for you soon, Brianna, soon beloved, and you will know our touch in truth, as well as in dreams.*

* * * * *

"…you will know our touch in truth, as well as in dreams…" Brianna heard the whispered words as hands traveled sensually over her nude body.

Her nipples beaded as she moaned against the feel of a heated mouth enveloping them, a ghostly lick had her arching closer to the touch. Her hands clenched into the blankets, her thighs tightening, pressing together as she felt a peculiar caress between them. Gods. She tossed restlessly as phantom hands parted the lips of her sex, and a moist, liquid swipe of a patient tongue ran through the heated slit, then circled the throbbing, aching bud of her clit. Sensation gathered within her, pulling at her, drawing her deeper into pleasure, closer to paradise.

She was awash in heated need. She pressed her breasts closer to the warmth of male hands, knowing the danger, knowing even in sleep that it was Drago's lips feeding voraciously at her nipples, and Lasan's tongue, patient and sure, that lapped at the slick moisture between her thighs.

Even in sleep, beneath the spell of their magick touch, she knew the differences. Knew who touched where, whose magick warmed her breasts, and whose lips suckled at her throbbing clit. Whose fingers were sliding tentatively, gently into…

"Wake up! Wake up, Princess! Their evil is infecting you. Sly, merciless bastards. Wake up now, I say!" A vicious pinch on her tender arm and the coarse, fearful voice of her old nurse had Brianna jerking awake.

Fear washed over her. Brilliant blue and green coils of magick wrapped around her body. They were beautiful. So velvety soft as they caressed her, filled her with warmth and desire. She felt adored…

"Trickery. Evil is what they beget," Elspeth snarled as she pinched Brianna again, her expression filled with terror. "Block them, Princess. Stop them now before they tear you apart with their magick alone."

As the nurse ranted, she felt a warmth probing with soft insistence at her vagina. She shuddered in pleasure, her body wracked by heat and need. She could feel a pressure building, an uncontrollable surge of such sensation she nearly cried aloud. Her eyes widening, Brianna fought the blankets that twisted around her body as well. She cried out in fear as she felt that warmth, a magick caress, a tender probing at the tightly closed bud of her anus.

She fought desperately for the words that would block the Wizards so daring as to send their touch across the distance that separated her. Her hands reached out to draw the magick that lived in the very air she breathed. She called on the Sorceress Matriarch, on the divinely female goddess who would protect her. As weak as even her fledgling power was, it was enough to allow her to break free of their hold and to jump from the bed.

She watched, almost with regret, as the magick coils slowly dissipated, then disappeared, once again a part of the land and the air around her.

"They are strong." She trembled, turning to Elspeth as she twisted her hands together worriedly. "They weren't cruel, Elspeth…"

"Do you think I lie?" Elspeth's voice was harsh, furious. Her expression was drawn into pinched lines of hatred as she faced Brianna. "Would I lie about my own child? How I held her, broken and bleeding to her death, a victim of their foul magick?"

Brianna shook her head desperately. She remembered Elspeth's daughter, once a playmate to herself and her sisters. The small, shy girl had possessed an endearing grin, but a shadow of fear always darkened her eyes. She seemed wary around her mother, though Elspeth has always been kind and gentle to Brianna and her sisters. The girl's death had been terribly upsetting to Brianna and the house of Sellane. The brutal rape was laid at the door of Wizard Twins, though there was no proof to be found that any had traveled to the lands of the Covenani.

"No, Elspeth, you wouldn't lie," she whispered, but she wondered. A small warning ember of suspicion flared inside her. "I will go sleep with Marina tonight," she continued, breathing harshly. "They cannot find me there, that close to Mother."

Elspeth took a deep, hard breath. Her wrinkled features were slowly easing, the fanatic, hard gleam in her eyes softening. She nodded her graying head firmly.

"You will do this. Go to your mother, tell her that the bastards assault you in your own bed," Elspeth ordered. "The monsters think to force an alliance with you. To destroy your innocent body. I will protect you from this, my Princess. No matter the cost, I will protect you."

Brianna backed away from the sudden flame of fury that flared once again in the aging woman's pale eyes. Elspeth watched her slyly, carefully. Brianna grabbed her robe and, leaving her slippers, rushed from the bedroom.

Her body still hummed with arousal, and she could still feel the faint touch of the Twins' magick even now, despite the spell of protection. The Sorceress Matriarch was pledged to protect her from dark evil. She was Covenani. If the Veraga Twins were such monsters, why did she still feel their touch, soothing now, comforting?

She could feel their bodies like a phantom presence, tall, broad and muscular, pressed against her. They were truly gifted with a physique that would turn any woman's eye. They stood shoulders and head above her, their large frames nearly dwarfing her. Wide shoulders and taut abdomens, strong, powerful legs. The thought of their legs had her shivering with arousal and fear. She remembered well the thick growth between those legs last year, during her mother's visit to the Cauldaran lands.

They had pressed against her, their cocks so hard, so hot, they seared her skin through the clothing that separated them. Her breathing escalated further. Gods, they should not excite her so. They were monsters. Creatures without caring. And now they invaded her dreams, her sleep, using her body, her female needs against her. They would destroy her, just as they had destroyed Elspeth's daughter.

She shuddered in fear and rushed for the safety of her mother's rooms. As Queen, her powers were much stronger, her protective shields thicker. Surely her mother would heed her pleas now, and no longer allow the courtship the Veraga Twins were pressing. Surely now, her mother would see the dangers. She had to...

Why an electronic book?

We live in the Information Age—an exciting time in the history of human civilization, in which technology rules supreme and continues to progress in leaps and bounds every minute of every day. For a multitude of reasons, more and more avid literary fans are opting to purchase e-books instead of paper books. The question from those not yet initiated into the world of electronic reading is simply: *Why?*

1. ***Price.*** An electronic title at Ellora's Cave Publishing and Cerridwen Press runs anywhere from 40% to 75% less than the cover price of the exact same title in paperback format. Why? Basic mathematics and cost. It is less expensive to publish an e-book (no paper and printing, no warehousing and shipping) than it is to publish a paperback, so the savings are passed along to the consumer.
2. ***Space.*** Running out of room in your house for your books? That is one worry you will never have with electronic books. For a low one-time cost, you can purchase a handheld device specifically designed for e-reading. Many e-readers have large, convenient screens for viewing. Better yet, hundreds of titles can be stored within your new library—on a single microchip. There are a variety of e-readers from different manufacturers. You can also read e-books on your PC or laptop computer. (Please note that Ellora's Cave does not endorse any specific brands.

You can check our websites at www.ellorascave.com or www.cerridwenpress.com for information we make available to new consumers.)

3. ***Mobility***. Because your new e-library consists of only a microchip within a small, easily transportable e-reader, your entire cache of books can be taken with you wherever you go.
4. ***Personal Viewing Preferences.*** Are the words you are currently reading too small? Too large? Too... ANNOYING? Paperback books cannot be modified according to personal preferences, but e-books can.
5. ***Instant Gratification.*** Is it the middle of the night and all the bookstores near you are closed? Are you tired of waiting days, sometimes weeks, for bookstores to ship the novels you bought? Ellora's Cave Publishing sells instantaneous downloads twenty-four hours a day, seven days a week, every day of the year. Our webstore is never closed. Our e-book delivery system is 100% automated, meaning your order is filled as soon as you pay for it.

Those are a few of the top reasons why electronic books are replacing paperbacks for many avid readers.

As always, Ellora's Cave and Cerridwen Press welcome your questions and comments. We invite you to email us at Comments@ellorascave.com or write to us directly at Ellora's Cave Publishing Inc., 1056 Home Avenue, Akron, OH 44310-3502.

ELLORA'S CAVE
ROMANTICA PUBLISHING